SHINY THING

SHINY THING

ISBN 978-1-907881-09-1

Papaveria Press

Acknowledgements:

"Dear, Dear" first published in *Scheherezade's Bequest* March 2008
"Fugly" first published in the anthology *Zencore*, edited by D.F. Lewis
"Grandpa Lost his Toothbrush" first published in *A Cappella Zoo*, Issue 1
"Happyfacing" first published in *Dog versus Sandwich* June 2008
"How Not to Apologize to a Scarecrow" first published in *City Slab* #8
"In Comes I" first published in *Tales of the Unanticipated* #27
"Lusard Street" first published in *Surreal* #1
"Redemption" first published in *Tales of the Unanticipated* #26
"Shiny Thing" first published in *City Slab* #6
"Soft Child" first published in *City Slab* #4
"The Children are to Blame" first published in *Tales of the Unanticipated* #25
"The Jaculi" first published in *Tales of the Unanticipated* #29
"The Ogre's Wife" first published in *Tales of the Unanticipated* #27
"The Old Husband's Tale" first published in *Talebones* #35
"Turning, or Turning" first published in *ChiZine* #45

PAPAVERIA PRESS

www.papaveria.com

If you're playing with magic and you try to cheat, you are one hundred per cent sure to get screwed.

SHINY THING

PATRICIA RUSSO

Table of Contents

Dear, Dear

❦

The boy was trashed, or worse. Drunk, stoned, or mentally challenged—the only three options. A double whammy was not impossible, however, nor even a triple one. The kid wore grimy wind pants and a flannel shirt with the sleeves torn off; he crouched in the stairwell, his back against the wall, hugging something to his chest, crooning to it. There was no cup or upturned cap by his feet, but he glanced at everyone coming down the steps, trying to make eye contact. In the piss-colored light, his face looked dead. Lips moved in the corpse-face, a cracked voice chanted in monotonous rhythm: "This is my child, my dear, dear child, who will not grow, who will not thrive." Some garbage from a poem, sounded like. His shirt was unbuttoned, and he was clutching it, whatever it was, against his chest, up close to his left nipple. "My dear, dear child, who will not grow, who will not thrive." Certainly not a baby; the head was the wrong shape, triangular, like a folded newspaper, and the body much too bumpy and lumpy under the grimy dishtowel the kid'd draped over it. Alive, though. It moved. Maybe. Or perhaps it was just the quivering of the kid's scrawny chest, the pulse of his heart and the piston of his breaths, that made it seem to move. You put your hand on my arm and said, "Don't laugh," squeezing hard, "don't laugh at him, he loves it," as we hurried down the steps to the platform and the train.

Lusard Street

YESTERDAY MORNING, SHORTLY BEFORE NOON, AS I WAS heading down to Lusard Street to kill you, I turned left at south end of March Avenue to avoid a crowd of hand-clapping, lash-bearing fools. Springtime invariably draws the insane back to the city. (Who had said that? Ah, yes, that was one of yours, its shallowness characteristic of your quips, its origin one of your infrequent introspective moments, for of course you, too, had first come to the city in the spring.) Passersby had already gathered to jeer, and the noise and the blood jangled my nerves. So I made the turn, and walked up a street I had never taken before, though I've lived in the city twenty years.

The day was clear, and warm for the season, as it had been for several days. Today the chill has returned, and there is ice in the basin on my washstand. All is change, all is chance. Yesterday, I was not wearing my jacket. I thought to put it on, the brown one you hate so, before setting off, but I knew I would have to walk the whole way and decided not to subject myself to a sweatbath. Your horrible, airless studio would be hot enough. I wished to arrive at your doorstep cool, if not calm.

I turned. I took a way I had never taken before.

I had not gone two steps before a dog leaped at me from nowhere and snapped its teeth down on my right arm. The dog was huge, with something of the wolf in him, and gaunt, and I thought I was about to die on that filthy street, with the stink of a nearby trash fire burning in my nose, the whistles of the flagellants' whips on March Avenue in my ears.

The dog's head reached to my waist; its eyes met mine with a cool, yellow gaze. It made a soft sound, not a growl, and began to drag me forward. The thing crawled with fleas; I could see them leaping and skittering through its thin fur. The sight of the vermin made me cry out, as the sudden sharp pinch of the dog's jaws had not, and I raised my free hand to hit it. The animal was a skeleton in a sack of skin, but it was maniacally strong and my arm felt as if it were in the grip of a jagged vise. A wet vise; the creature's saliva ran freely, and my sleeve was already soaked with it. A new fear hit me, for I had read the journals as well as you, those nights in the coffee house, and I thought, *Only a scratch from those teeth, even if the beast lets me go, the least break in the skin and it can be death, a death of torment and thirst and raving.* And I thought, as it continued to pull me forward, past an abandoned cart that had been stripped of its wheels, past shuttered doors, over refuse that had escaped, charred but unconsumed, from the most recent communal trash fire, how fortunate the ignorant were, who only trembled at devils.

We had gone far, the dog and I, though we had taken only a few steps. The smell of fire, of blackened wood and ash, was thick in the air, but it was an old scent, dampened by time and the rain that had fallen two nights ago. The fire that had burned here had not been set by the local inhabitants to clear some of the garbage from the alleys and back streets, as sometimes happens in your neighborhood, but had been a conflagration of dwelling places, taking four or five of the closely-built structures, consuming the interiors, leaving only their stone skins, charred and cracked like the carnival masks my father had once burnt in a fit of piety. I saw where the fire must have started, in the middle tenement of the consumed row. That building had suffered most; its roof was gone, and the exterior walls, though of stone, as was required by the rules of the city, had collapsed. The buildings on either side leaned toward the vacancy between them; their walls, too, would fall soon. The only building that seemed outwardly sound was the one before which the dog halted. I could no longer hear the cries of the fanatics on the avenue. I could no longer feel my arm; below the elbow the flesh was numb, which put me in mind of subtler poisons, of creatures bred in glass cases and reared on small but ever-increasing doses of venom, until every pore of their being oozed the toxin they themselves were unscathed by, beings innocuous to the eye, who could kill with a breath. You had told me such a tale, once, then the next morning denied having recounted it.

I heard a scraping sound, and a small noise like water trickling, or sand running out of a broken clock.

The dog whimpered, then woofed softly, without opening its mouth. It had never taken its cool yellow eyes off me, not for an instant.

The charred building's windows were blank and open, the shutters torn off or consumed, the glass shattered or melted, if glass indeed had ever graced them, the curtains gone to ash. The front door had been smashed off its hinges; it lay, not yet filched and broken up for some cook stove, splintered and trampled on the pavement. The dog skirted it without a glance. A miraculous dog, this, even with a touch of the wolf in it, which could starve for a season and yet maintain the strength of a bull, which could walk backwards through a narrow, winding, waste-strewn street and never stumble, never falter.

It wanted me to enter the burnt, derelict tenement. Now, it pulled at me harder, with increased urgency, almost yanking me off my feet. The scraping, trickling sound came from within the building. In the air, gray particles danced. The sun was at noon, and light shone down into the alley. Stone dust, I thought, and I thought, a mad mason at work inside there, or even worse, a sculptor. But I heard no metal, no clink of tools.

Then I caught the scent of the second sort of dust in the air, and I stopped dead. The dog's teeth scraped over my skin. That was it, then; were the animal rabid, no ointment or poultice could draw the evil out, no cauterization, however severe, could stay it.

The dog growled, fiercely.

A woman appeared in the doorway of the ruined building. A ruined woman, for a ruined building; her face and its façade were well matched. In a cracked, dry, powdery voice, she said, "Odel."

The dog stopped growling. Its tail began to wag with improbable glee. Still, it kept its eyes on me, fixedly.

"Good dog," the woman said, tenderly. Then, to me, she said, "I beg your pardon."

Young, old, it was impossible to tell. Her face was cratered, furrowed; powder flew off her cheeks when she spoke. Her clothing, which covered her decently from chin to fingertips to feet, was heavy with it. Her hair was dark, but that meant nothing. Her eyes were dark, as well, and grown large. Exposed. The skin and the sockets that protected them had crumbled away. No eyelids now, I did not think. It was clear that she was far gone; when the complaint reached the eyes, the end was said to be near. It was also said that the powdering of the eyes caused the sufferer the most pain, far beyond that caused by the affliction of any other bodily parts. You made a rude joke on that subject once, and I laughed along with the rest. This woman, though, in her loose, toe-length, long-sleeved dress, was stoic. Perhaps, though, her lack of emotion was merely a sign that she could no longer cry.

"I granulate," she said, and I nodded. We in the city had long since ceased to pretend that the malady was confined to those unfortunates compelled to make their habitation or earn their livelihood in the South Quarter, but still, never to that moment, never until yesterday, had I met a sufferer.

"Please come in," she said. "I need your help."

"Madam—" My own voice was cracked, and dry as chalk.

"Not for myself. For another."

The dog wagged its tail, and growled softly.

"Odel, no," she said.

"You have a well-trained animal," I said, for now I saw that the dog's actions had all been purposeful, bent to a goal not its own, but hers.

"Odel has great understanding," she said, nodding slightly. More powder tumbled. "Once he shared my bed, went bathing with me, ate morsels off my plate. He has stayed with me faithfully, though now I cannot even so much as stroke him." She must have seen something in my face, surprise perhaps, or dismay, for she added, "I was not always like this, you know." She stepped back from the doorway, disappearing into the interior of the burnt building. The dog, its tail still waving cheerfully, dragged me forward, onward, over the threshold and inside.

Within, all was shards and ash, splinters and destruction. While, by centuries-old ordinance, every structure in the city must have its exterior constructed of stone, there is no law to dictate how the builders throw together the insides. We joked about that, too, once, didn't we? Wood, wood, always wood, and the cheapest at that. One spark catching a curtain at an open window, one cinder falling on a threadbare rug, and all is conflagration, walls, floors, stairs, ceiling. The exterior of this building still stood, but within it had been scoured hollow. Furniture and belongings, pans and shirts, a warped frame missing its portrait, broken crockery and blackened books, lay in heaps all around, fallen from above. I tipped my head back. I could see straight up to the underside of the roof.

"Here," the woman said, but I was looking elsewhere, at a cleared spot in the rubble, a clean space from which all the detritus had carefully been pushed back, and in the center of which a porcelain doll lay. The doll reposed on her back, her worn and darned pinafore smoothed down, modestly, to her knees. She must have been an expensive doll once, when new, for her eyes were of blue glass and her hair clearly human. The paint had gone from her face, but her lips curved in a gentle smile. And well might she smile, for beside her lay a plate of fresh cakes, and a full bottle of old wine.

"My mother," the woman who granulated said, "before she died, gave me that doll. If ever you are in trouble, she said, if ever you are in difficulty, if ever you are at a loss, then feed the doll, feed it well, and then heed its advice."

"You feed the doll," I said, looking at the dog, with its bones protruding from its skin.

"I do."

"And it advises you?"

"She led me here. She told me about this," and the woman touched her hand to a wall. A stone wall, the building's exterior wall, well-built by strict regulation, a foot thick at the very least. In every place other than where she stood, the surviving stone walls of the place were dark gray with soot. Where the woman placed her hand, the wall had been cleaned. The stone, what remained, was white.

Under her hand, the stone began, slowly, to granulate, and the granules to fall, with painful lethargy, to the floor. She had been working away at this wall for quite some time, it was clear. Even in the final grip of the illness, she did not granulate quickly. The stone powdered slowly, slowly, slowly. I could count a hundred heartbeats between the fall of one grain and the next. She had managed to create a shallow declivity in the stone wall, a thumb deep, perhaps, but it must have taken her ages.

She spread her fingers, wiped straight down, angrily. The stone did not degrade, did not granulate, any more quickly.

"There is something alive in here," she said.

The woman was about to die. Even as I stared at her, uncomprehendingly, her hand, the one she had just passed over the wall, turned into tiny crumbs of dry matter and spattered to the floor. She let out a long breath. I held my own, though it was much too late. If, as some thought, the malady might be communicated by the exhalations of the afflicted, then within a week I, too, would begin to granulate.

The dog was still gripping my arm.

It was absurd. There are only so many deaths one may face without bursting into laughter. Evisceration by a starving wolf, a year of rabid agony, months of desiccating granulation... I was overcome. I laughed. I doubled over. I laughed until I was nearly sick.

"There is something alive in here," the woman repeated, calmly. I could not fathom her calmness, though after a moment, after I regained a modicum of self-mastery, I admired it. One day, perhaps, if I live, I may attain such control of myself. "It lives, and I will free it. But I need your help."

I never imagined she was mad, never for a moment. Madness was not one of the symptoms of the granulating illness.

"Your dog is starving," I said. "And yet your doll is sated."

"I will free this living thing," she went on, as remorselessly, as unheedingly, as a cart trundling over a stray child. "But I cannot touch it, as you well know. Should I touch it, it will turn to dust and powder and arid nothingness. I will wear away the wall to the last stratum. But you must break through it, so the thing may live."

"Else?" I asked.

"Else Odel shall tear out your throat."

She was very serious, yet I could not stop laughing. Piqued, she turned and ran her left hand, her only whole one now, down the wall, and long moments later, another layer of stone turned to dust and fell at her feet.

I laughed and laughed, until I heard something fluttering, or perhaps squirming, within the wall.

That sound stilled me.

You always mocked my hearing, how I mistook one voice for another's, how I could not decipher whispers in a crowded, noisy room. I wish you had been beside me yesterday. You would not have mocked then.

"What," I said, very softly, and then my voice failed me.

"It wishes to be born," the dying woman said. "As all living things do. You must help me. You must help it."

"Or else your wolf will rip out my throat?"

There was a silence. From her, from me. In the muteness between us, the susurration of falling granules was as loud as thunder. Beneath it, the flutter. The scratch. The rubbing against hard, unforgiving rock.

I began to believe.

"Odel," she said. "Come."

The terrible dog released me. Instantly, with no hesitation, no worried glance at its mistress. It dashed to her, the woman who was losing herself grain by grain, who was dying mote by mote, and took up a wary guard post at her side. At a distance. Beyond arm's reach.

A miraculous dog. A genius among dogs.

I could have run. Perhaps the dog would not have caught me. It was starving, after all. Had been starving for quite some long time. Perhaps it had expended all its meticulously harbored store of energy in capturing me, in compelling me, inch by dragged inch, to come to this place.

The woman had only one hand now.

She drew her remaining hand down the wall one more time. After an eternity, stone turned to granules, and granules fell. I almost cried.

"What is it?" I asked, and she shook her head, as far as she was able. I understood, but, stupidly, could not halt my tongue. "What will it become, then?"

She conserved her breath. Once more, but more slowly, she guided her hand down the wall.

And now, I could see movement behind the thin screen of stone. "All right," I said, "all right," though even then, even at that moment, I did see that the living thing trapped inside the stone was horrible.

She smiled at me, or I thought she smiled. She smiled as far as she was able. She stepped aside. I stepped forward.

"Wait," I said, "no, it's not enough, I can't," because I did not want to touch the creature, even glancingly. The stone was thin now, a layer barely the thickness of a fingernail. The thing within was coiled and serpentine, spiked and furred, and eager for freedom. It hurled itself against the stone, and I recoiled. It was dreadful. It was revolting. It was ugly.

The woman raised her hand, and I cried out, "But it's disgusting."

"It's alive," she said. "That's enough." Coming forward, she ran her hand down the wall once again. We waited until the crumbles of matter finished dropping, and then I struck the remaining layer of stone with my fist.

It shattered. Shards of stone flew, cutting my hand, cutting my face.

The thing inside drew breath, and screamed.

The dog wagged its tail. The damn animal, with its tongue lolling and white teeth glinting, looked to be grinning.

The thing in the wall emerged. It pulled itself out of the hole I had made with hooked, black, finger-long talons. Its eyes, slit like a cat's but four times as large, blinked rapidly in the light. Its eyes were gray. Its skin was pale rose. Out of the dry wall, freed by a dry, granulating woman, it heaved forward, slick as salad oil, and glistening.

It was the most hideous object I had ever had the misfortune to see. Humped, crooked, the pale rose skin dimming almost instantly to a dull, dead coal-ash, its initial smoothness scabbing over, scaling, as soon as the air touched it, this new creature, this impossible neonate, seemed part serpent, part scorpion (for it possessed eight legs, I saw, as it came fully out of the hole, and hairy legs at that), and part sewer rat. It had a mouth, more or less in the center of its narrow, spade-shaped head. Clinging to the wall, face downward, it gaped that mouth open, wide, wider, as wide as two hand spans, and gulped air.

I must have scuttled back. Must have, though I was unaware of my own movements. I was across the room, my back against a sooty wall, heaps of broken and burnt furnishings between myself and the newborn, and yet I shrank down, covered my head with my arms, and shook like one in the grip of an ague.

The woman, and the dog, stood to the side, and watched. The dog was silent, motionless. The woman smiled. So I was wrong about her inability to express emotion, I thought. She smiled, as broadly as any healthy person, and clasped the stump of her right hand in the palm of her left, and nodded encouragement to the dreadful creature as it leaped to the floor, shook itself like a damp chicken, and then took its first tentative steps toward the world. "Go," she said, her voice dry and cracked, and joyful. "Be well."

"It's horrible," I said. "It's detestable, disgusting. It's wrong."

"It's alive," she answered. "Surely the detestable and disgusting also have the right to live?"

Those were the last words I heard her speak. The monster born from the wall scrambled out into the daylight. A few moments later, when I had gathered my wits to take my own first step toward the exit, the woman did not stay me. The dog remained at her side. Both of them were silent, as if deep in thought.

Even when I returned, almost an hour later, the two of them, woman and dog, kept their silence. In the interim, she had managed to sit down, and rest her head on her knees. The dog lay on its side, a foot or so from her. Close, but not too close. The dog raised its head as I entered, and sniffed the air.

I set down my basket and my bundle, and turned to go, but then thought again, and knelt to unwrap the scraps of meat I had begged from the butcher whose daughter I had once tutored in the mysteries of the alphabet. In the basket there was bread, two days old and stolen, as was the basket itself. (I am not as old as you think me; I can still snatch and run.) Let her stir herself, I thought; if she's hungry enough, if she wants to live a bit longer, she will rise and come to eat; she can feed herself. But the meat I tossed to the dog, to forestall any chance of the woman taking the notion to feed the bits of gristle and sinew to her damned and damnable doll.

The dog devoured every morsel, and licked its chops, and wagged its tail at me.

The woman sat with her head on her knees, and never stirred. That night, half asleep, I suddenly started, and thought: perhaps she was dead, perhaps she had died in the interval between my departure from the ruined building and my return, and I, foolishly, as I am often foolish, had not noticed. Alone in my bed, I was stabbed by anguish, inane, asinine, but as sharp as a wolf's tooth, as stinging as a flagellant's whip. There was no way to know for sure. Certainly, I would not go back to that hollowed-out tenement. I would not look for her. But in my memory I marked that on her patch of floor the woman had sat as motionless as the doll had lain on hers.

And as for you, I did not kill you yesterday. It seemed to me, yesterday, that there was sufficient death in this world. That one new thing had been born did not tip the scales, so heavily weighted in favor of the old enemy, even a trifle. It seems to me I shall not kill you today. I feel a bit unwell. Over-excitement, over-exertion. My constitution has never been robust. You would mock me for that failing often, do you not recall? And I believe I shall not kill you tomorrow. But there are many, many days left to me, and to you as well, and I cannot tell whether or when my mood will change, so I make you no promise that one fine morning I shall not awaken with fresh resolve and renewed hatred, and set forth with determination to Lusard Street, to take your life.

The Children are to Blame

"You don't really mean that," Zach said, smiling that small pursey-lipped smile. It was the expression of his I liked the least. "Nobody really hates kids."

Zach was an active, outdoorsy guy. He had to be stretching and straining, sweating buckets, if not popping ligaments, to be happy. The idea of sitting indoors with a fat newspaper on a Sunday afternoon made him itch all over. He'd wanted to go rock climbing, claimed he knew a great spot, two hours drive out of town, swore it would be worth it. I'd wanted to catch up on the crap happening in the world, work the crossword puzzle, polish off the contents of all the take-out cartons that had piled up in the fridge since Monday. I swore team crossword solving was just as good as foreplay and elderly rice might get crusty but it wouldn't make you sick. We compromised on a stroll in the park.

Zach, big surprise, insisted on taking the nature trails. Nobody else in the damn park ever bothered with them. Cyclists and bladers stuck to the nice smooth asphalt lane loosely cinching the lake. Dog walkers crunched over the gravelled paths. Picnickers and Frisbee-snappers laid claim to the grassy areas, with the soccer players relegated to less desirable bare-dirt stretches. A place for everyone and everyone in their place. Except for Zach and me, alone on the stupid nature trail. Alone if you didn't count the millions of gnats hovering in low, buzzing clouds, eager to suck our sweat, or the occasional rabbit we startled or squirrel we pissed off. But as this was a compromise—at least we weren't rock climbing—I tried to cling to a positive attitude and appreciate the privacy thing—we could strip naked and make love hanging from a couple of branches with no one to notice but the gnats. And I was managing it, enjoying myself despite the sweating, enjoying Zach, enjoying his enjoyment, until the trail, which must have taken a couple of weird kinks when I wasn't paying attention, opened up and suddenly we were smack dab outside the playground.

"Shit," I said. Why hadn't I heard the yelling, that distinctive high-pitched eardrum-drilling blood-vessel-bursting polyphonous shriek children emit whenever more than one of them is plopped down somewhere. Too many no-see-ums clogging my ears. Too much of Zach, on my skin, in my nose (deep, I liked to inhale him, his sweat smelled spicy), in my brain. "Let's turn around. Come on. I want to go back."

He didn't hear me. Totally zoned out, grooving on the kids, with this sappy expression on his face. I turned so I wasn't facing the playground head on, but I could still catch movement, flashes of color, in my peripheral vision. "Zach!"

"Aren't they great?" he said, dreamily.

"No."

"I love kids," he went on, in the same syrupy, brain-damaged sort of tone. "They're so in touch with the world. So *there*. Centered, you know? So alive. Someday I want a house full of kids. Like six or eight." He grinned at this fantasy. "That'd be so cool."

"Can we go now?" I said, icily.

"What's up with you?"

"I hate kids. I've told you that before. I'd be very happy if I never had to see or hear or smell a single one of those selfish snot-nosed brats again in my life. And yeah, yeah, I know, we're living in the real world, it's not possible *never* to deal with kids. But I do my fucking best, Zach. So let's go."

A beat, two beats. Then Zach smiled his knowing little smile and informed me that I didn't really mean it.

PATRICIA RUSSO

"I do mean it. I despise children."

"You were a child yourself once."

"I know," I said. That was the problem.

Zach shook his head, very slowly. "You never want to have kids?"

"Never."

"You'll change your mind."

"Don't hold your breath," I said, and strode past him, back to the stupid nature trail. It took a moment, but he did follow me.

"I gotta say, I don't get it," he said, mournfully. "Kids are the future. Kids are life. The most precious things on this planet. Okay, so, I know there's the responsibility and everything, and the money, right, it's real expensive to have a kid these days, but come on. For real. Children are what make it all worthwhile."

"Children are death," I said.

"Oh, stop it."

We were in the dappled shade again, the leaves rustling above us, the gnats humming, the squirrels doing their furious chut-chut-chuttering.

"Oh," he said, suddenly. "This is about where you grew up? That slummy place?"

A slum, and worse than a slum, but there was magic there. Had been, I mean. There had been magic there once.

"So, is that the story? You had a crappy childhood?" Zach asked, impatiently. "Six kids in a bed, cockroaches as pets? No heat, lead paint flaking off the walls? Drugs, booze, police helicopters landing on your street?"

I was silent. We walked for a while.

"Your parents," he said. "Your parents weren't great."

"My parents were wonderful," I said.

☙

They should have killed me at birth.

Dad worked the night shift, maintenance staff at a hospital. Mom had lots of different jobs, usually two or three at once. Cleaning homes, offices. Pick-and-pack in warehouses. Factory work, filling boxes, punching out plastic. Once she worked in a donut shop and used to come home smelling of powdered sugar. I liked that.

Some parts of the city weren't too bad. Where the community college was, that was okay, and the area everybody called The Heights had nice houses with front lawns and circular driveways. We didn't live in one of those parts.

I remember the sun shining into the room where we slept, not through the window, which was taped over with cardboard and plastic bags to keep out the cold, but through the crack in the wall up near the ceiling. We were living on the top floor of an old house that had been divided up into apartments. Where we slept used to be the attic, with the duck-or-you'll-crack-your-skull ceilings to prove it. Freezing in winter, stifling in summer. No place to play, any time, because the streets were too dangerous and the public school chased everybody out of the cement courtyard at three-thirty and locked up the gates. We had a TV, but if we played it too loud the folks downstairs started banging on their ceiling with a broom handle.

When I was sick Mom would sleep next to me, and my sisters would have to scrunch all together, muttering and complaining, at the other end. But she did the same for them when they were sick. Six in a bed… Zach had it almost right. There were four of us, all girls, and for a long time we were all small enough to sleep on one mattress laid out on the floor. A long time. Almost forever. We were all still little when the magic came.

I remember whenever I got scared Dad would hold me and whisper in my ear that it'd be okay, not because there was nothing to be afraid of, because he knew that there damn well was, but because I was strong and smart and whatever scary thing came at me, I'd beat it. He whispered to my sisters, too. I don't know if he gave them the same words he gave me. That was something too private to ask about.

At night rats boogied in the walls and street kids shot each other over the best dope-dealing spots. Sometimes weird creatures climbed out of the sewers and snatched little kids off the curb. That wasn't magic, though. Mrs. Valzano, who was circus-lady fat and had taught third grade for a thousand years, said she was surprised that sort of stuff didn't happen more often, what with all the different factories dumping chemicals down there. And the meatpacking plants, too. Flush enough blood and chemicals into one place, let 'em swirl around, maybe ferment a little, maybe get hit by a sharp bolt of lightning one hot summer night, and shit will occur. That was science, said Mrs. Valzano.

Dad had a mustache and big hands with hard, knobbly knuckles. He used to brush his teeth with baking soda instead of toothpaste. He didn't like baseball, but he loved to watch science programs, especially the ones about stars and planets and the universe. Maybe that's why he always took night-shift work, so he could step outside and look at the stars on his breaks.

Mom had a streak of real toughness and a different talent in each of her hands. The left hand did hair, four little girls' hair as well as her own, in less time than it took most folks to find their brush and comb. The right one buttoned buttons solo, tied knots without help, and drew pictures. She drew a picture of the place where the magic appeared, once. I found it after she died. The paper had been crumpled up, then straightened out again, and hidden in the bottom of a drawer, under a pile of socks without partners and stretched-out bras.

Maybe she drew a lot of those pictures but only kept the one. I don't know.

"Jaynie, watch your sisters," Mom said. Jaynie was my name then. Since I was the oldest, I heard this a lot. But recently Mom had been going out at night, after Dad left for work. Leaving us alone. We were used to being alone for a couple of hours after school, but being alone at night was different. When my sisters saw Mom putting on her shoes, they immediately started to fuss. Mom got steely, then. "I love you girls," she said. "You all are my heart. But don't ruin this for me."

As soon as she shut the door behind her, dread settled on my chest like a stone.

The magic had come in the wintertime. For a long time none of us kids knew about it, because it was between the rusty dumpsters behind the chicken place near the freeway that had been out of business for years. Squatters lived in the old chicken place, and sometimes the women who worked on the street corners would take men in there, so even the older kids generally stayed away from it, except the ones that liked to start fires. I had no idea where Mom was going, but even the first time she left us, I got scared right down to the insides of my bones, and Dad wasn't there to tell me that whatever it was, I was strong enough to deal with it.

If there's a fire we'll die, I thought that first time.

A burglar could break in and kill us.

The horrible downstairs neighbors could rush up and kick in the door, shove pillowcases over our heads and tie up our arms and legs, drag us to the freeway overpass and throw us over, like that wino some high school boys did throw off the overpass who got hit in midair by the cab of a semi and burst like a balloon.

I could get sick and Mommy wouldn't be there.

Children are so selfish. I, I, I, all the time. Constantly.

Incessantly. Eternally. I want. I need. I have to have. Give me. Feed me. Look at me. Tend me. Love me.

Makes me puke.

My little sisters cried and said there was a bear in the closet and I smacked them. I made them go to bed early, but I left the light on, and I decided I'd stay up, no matter what, no matter how late it got, or what weird noises I heard, or how many rats ran across my damn feet, until Mom got home. But of course I fell asleep, and when I woke up I was under the covers with my sisters and Dad was back from the night shift and Mom was making breakfast.

Night after night, Mom went out.

And then Dad started not coming home in the morning. Mom would be there, telling us to hurry up and get ready for school, but Dad wouldn't. And Mom would have a tiny, almost invisible smile on her face, an expression she'd never worn before. Mom had always smiled with all her teeth. Now when she looked at us, her eyes were as flat as pennies. When she touched me, electricity sparked off her skin and made every one of my hairs stand on end.

Soon Dad stopped going to work at all. He and Mom started leaving the apartment together. First they wouldn't come back for hours. Then they weren't coming back for days, and we were alone, my little sisters and me, washing our underwear in the bathroom sink, not combing our hair, screaming at the ghosts we saw in the shadows, playing with the burner on the stove, huddling under all the blankets and our coats too when the heat went off and didn't come on again. Eating dry cereal and scraping the peanut butter jar. Breaking a glass. Bleeding. Fighting over the TV, stabbing each other with forks because we weren't allowed to handle knives. Bleeding. Running into the bathroom door and blacking my eye. Not going to school anymore. Not watching TV anymore. Not even crying anymore. Not doing much but lying curled up on the mattress under all the coats and blankets.

I didn't want to believe Mom and Dad had gone to the magic, too.

It took a while for us kids to find out about the magic coming, but the grown-ups couldn't keep the secret forever. They should have been more careful. But same as my mom and dad, the rest slipped up, started taking off for hours at a time, not showing up, not coming home. If they'd been a little more patient, a little more circumspect, possibly none of us would have caught on. They weren't, and we did. In school and out of school, it was all the kids were talking about: their mommas, their aunties, their dads, their grands. It was happening all over, even foster parents and group home staff. Gone for hours. Soon, gone for days. Naturally, some kids decided they were going to follow their grownups and find out what the story was. Naturally some of the kids were caught, chased back home before they learned anything. But just as naturally, a couple of the kids succeeded. And they told the rest of us.

And some of us went to look for ourselves.

Behind the out-of-business chicken place, where the dumpsters were, there used to be a parking lot. A shot-up sign still bolted to one of the surviving metal poles of the run-in, run-down, run-over, and run-through chain-link fence said Patrons Only. The place was full of junk now, shopping carts, beat up baby strollers, car batteries, all that kind of stuff. A whole bunch of people must have used the lot for a bathroom, too, because even though it had snowed at least three times that month, and it was so cold your snot made icicles on your upper lip, you could still smell it, number one and number two. It was bad when you were standing up, but a thousand times worse when you were crouching down behind a pile of snow-crusted garbage bags, keeping low so as not to be seen.

The first time I went, it was with a couple of kids from school. We didn't get too close. We just climbed up on one of the gritty, grimy snow-plow-created mountains outside the junk-lot and stretched our necks as far as we could.

The lot was full of grownups, waiting in line. The line curved and curved again, essing five or six times. All the grownups stood very still and very quiet. The line only moved once every ten minutes or so, it seemed like, but nobody talked. Nobody listened to headphones, or smoked a cigarette, or sipped a take-out coffee. Nobody even stamped their feet or shifted their weight or scratched their nose. It was cold, so cold, and none of them even shivered.

It was like they were waiting for something so important that they hardly dared to breathe in case they messed it up.

I was angry, so angry. Boiling mad, in that winter cold. There were so many people in the lot, all with their heads down and all so silent, that I couldn't tell if my mom and dad were among them, but it didn't matter. This is where they came, when they should have been home. This is what they did, when they were supposed to be taking care of me.

One of my friends from school said, "There's my Aunt Rosa," in a voice like he'd just got punched in the stomach.

We knew the grownups were lining up to squeeze into the space between two rusty dumpsters standing against the bare back wall of the old chicken place, but that time, the first time, I couldn't see what they did there.

Of course grownups did strange things all the time, without giving you reasons. Said you were too young to understand. You didn't believe it, of course. I remember fuming, stomping my feet, thinking, I *am* old enough to understand. I *am*.

But I wasn't, of course. None of us were, not even the big kids in high school. Maybe them the least, because they all thought they were going to live forever.

I went back, alone. To spy.

I found a way in under the ragged fence, my crawling progress concealed from the waiting adults by the heaps of junk and garbage bags piled up all around me. I feared if the grownups caught me there, they'd turn like a mob of wolves, tear me apart, legs, arms, and head all flying in different directions. But I was brave. I was determined. I was mad as hell. I wanted my mom and dad back.

The space between the dumpsters was about two feet wide. The snow had been cleared away, the concrete broken up and taken away, too. Between the dumpsters was only bare, brown dirt. From where I hid, face only a couple of inches from the frigid ground, breathing through my mouth and tasting urine, I had a perfect view. When one adult left the space, there was always a little pause before the next one went in. It was just dirt. Damn *dirt*. Plain, dry, winter soil, except that it was real brown, a deep, rich brown, like bittersweet chocolate, instead of the ashy gray you'd expect.

The little pause was because the grownup took off his or her clothes. All of them. Some people folded their coats and pants and underwear neatly and laid them carefully on the ground. Others just tore everything off and let their things drop anywhere.

Naked, the people stepped between the dumpsters and knelt on the ground. With their hands flat on the dirt, slowly, as if silently counting numbers off, they lowered their heads until their faces touched the ground. A shiver ran down their spines, one single long shiver, and no more. They stayed like that, unmoving, butts in the air and breasts and dicks hanging down, mouths on the dirt, inhaling slowly, exhaling even more slowly, for as long as they stayed there. Something must have told them when their time was up, and they rose, grabbed their clothes, got dressed, and left the lot.

That night I woke up and Mom and Dad were in the kitchen, talking softly, with one light on and their hands curled around cups of coffee; steam drifted up into their smooth, flat-eyed faces. Dad's hair had lost its crop of gray. Mom looked so much like the picture she saved from before she was married that I blinked.

Then the anger came in a rush, blinding me, and I shot out from under the blankets, savage, reckless, screaming. I flew into the kitchen, knocked the cup out of Mom's hand, spraying scalding liquid everywhere, kicked Dad in the leg, kicked him again, tried to slap them both; my hands were like wild birds, whipping through the air. My sisters woke up and started screaming, too, but all three of them stayed put on the mattress.

Dad grabbed me, scooped me up, held me tight to his chest. His face was kind. His eyes were flat and shiny.

Mom walked into the other room. "Hush," she said to my sisters.

They wouldn't listen. They wouldn't obey. They were not good children, either. My sisters cried and cried.

I squirmed in my father's arms, fighting, kicking him over and over. He began to rock me, but I butted his chin with the top of my head and bellowed, "Stop, stop it, stop it! I hate you! Don't go there any more!"

"You're too young to understand," he whispered in my ear. "Be a good girl, now."

"Hush," Mom was saying in the other room.

Both their voices sounded thin and faint. Dad was talking into my ear, but it felt like I was hearing him over a bad phone line in the middle of a storm.

Dad squeezed me. He held me tighter and tighter, until I stopped struggling and all the air was pressed out of my body and I couldn't get any more. When I was quiet he put me down on a kitchen chair. My sisters were still crying, but they stayed on the mattress, so Mom didn't squeeze them. Everything was sort of gray and I was coughing, and when I could see again I was lying on the floor. Guess I must've slipped off the chair. Mom and Dad had taken their coats and were gone.

Be a good girl, Dad said. But I wasn't. Once I started it, all the other kids joined in, but that doesn't make me feel any better. We were rotten, evil, all of us. Selfish little shits.

A few grownups, the ones who had first discovered the magic, the ones who'd been going to the back of the old chicken place the longest, were lucky. The magic had enough time to work on them all the way. My youngest sister still lives where we grew up. I don't talk to her much, but every once in a while my phone rings in the middle of the night and it'll be her on the other end, crying. Then I know she's seen one of the lucky people again. I don't hang up on her. I grip the receiver and listen to her weep. That is my punishment.

That winter, we kids killed the magic. And I was the first to begin.

I headed out with hate in my heart and fury hot as fever burning up my blood. My sisters came, too. We carried spoons, because that was all we could find to dig with, but as we made our way to the old chicken place some kids started to follow us. They knew. It was like an infection, jumping from me to my sisters then to each kid we saw, every kid we passed. They knew what we planned to do, and they rushed to do it with us. And some of these kids had spades, and some of these kids got hold of shovels.

At the lot, there were a few kids outside, watching. The infection caught them up and whirled them around; they started jumping up and down, shouting, their faces twisted into savagery. Animals. We were all rabid animals.

The adults waiting patiently and placidly in the lot had no chance. We swarmed them.

They were bigger than us, but we were wild.

They were many, but we were more.

They were our parents, and we gave them back to death.

Dad was right. We were too young to understand.

We swarmed in a frenzy like feeding sharks, over the torn and battered fence, under it, through it. Those with empty hands filled them with old umbrellas, lengths of corroded pipe, broken slats. We burst through the throng of adults, many of them now no longer quiet, no longer tranquil, but becoming alarmed, frightened, starting to shriek, beginning to awaken to the threat. We overwhelmed them with our speed and our fury and reached the back of the old chicken place, the rusty dumpsters, before any of the grownups could do more than start to snatch at us.

The adult hugging the earth between the dumpsters was a woman. She had gray hair. I think she worked in the cafeteria in my school. We were kids, and nudity scared us, but we dragged her out, by her naked ankles and her naked arms and her naked everything. She didn't know what was going on at first, but then she started to fight, and she got kicked in the face. That wasn't me. I didn't do that.

But I was the first one into the space between the dumpsters. Climbing over her shoulders. While she was being kicked. I reached the place first.

The ground was warm. Hot, like the outside of an oven. I stabbed my spoon into the dirt, and it went in easily. The earth was very dry and loose, like sand, and as I turned over the first spoonful, I smelled something tangy and sharp, like seaweed, like the ocean I'd seen just once, something deep and enveloping, something that swept out and wrapped around me for a second, tasting me, and then spit me out. I rocked back on my heels, hit with the worst nausea I ever felt in my life, my head spinning so bad I couldn't see. I spewed out everything in my stomach in one wrenching gush.

Then I stabbed the dirt again.

Then some other kids were crowding in, with their spades and pieces of pipe and bare hands, and we were digging up the ground frantically. Dirt flew everywhere, stinging my eyes. The adults were screaming like they were being slaughtered. The smaller kids, even those way in the back that never even got close to the dumpsters, were puking and messing themselves. It couldn't have been more than a few moments before I was shoved out of the space by the other kids, all of them fighting each other for the chance to get in on the kill. Like animals, snarling over carrion. Somebody whacked me in the chin. Somebody else bit my hand.

Mom and Dad were among the adults who'd been waiting in the lot. I saw them. They were screaming and trying to grab the shovels and things out of the hands of the rioting children, just like all the other grownups. Some of the kids went down. But there were more of us, more pouring into the lot every second, and we were wild.

In the end, it didn't take that much time.

Two or three feet of dirt, that was all that protected the magic from us. And when the dirt was removed, gone, thrown over shoulders, between legs, cast into the air and into the dumpsters and into our eyes and noses and mouths (for days, I tasted that dirt each time I swallowed…) and the magic was exposed to the air and to this world and to our small bloody filthy hands and to our hate, it died. From out of the hole we dug came an enormous exhalation, a long final breath that took the breath away from all of us and left everybody in the lot behind the old chicken place, kids and grownups both, stilled for an instant, then shaking. Then the stench swelled up and crashed over us, a bursting, swamping wave of putrefaction, stunning in its intensity, its completeness. A colossal thing had died, and its decay was colossal as well. There was nothing but rot in the world, and we were drowning in it.

So we fled.

PATRICIA RUSSO

Dad came back a couple of days after we killed the magic. Mom stayed away from us for a few weeks, but in the end she returned, too, and took up her life. We didn't talk about what had happened, what we had done, and as the months passed and then the years, on occasion it was even possible to forget it, until we caught a glimpse of one of the lucky people, and it all came back in a rush. I mean possible for the kids to forget. I don't imagine any of the adults ever did, not even for a second, not even in their dreams.

Mom died first, two strokes one after the other, the first one leaving her mute and twisted, the second carrying her off; Dad went harder, hooked up to IVs and catheters for months, his body getting thinner and thinner while his eyes grew bigger and bigger, until at the end he was a skeleton with enormous, accusing eyes that followed you wherever you went in the room. A lot of the other grownups who went to the magic are still alive, except the ones who started out old. Mom and Dad died young. Not everybody dies young. But everybody dies.

Except those few, those lucky, that handful of men and women who came across the magic first and managed to visit it enough times, put themselves into contact with it often enough. There aren't many, but they all still live there. Every once in a while, my youngest sister catches sight of one.

They are young. Not as young as children, of course, for that would be a curse, and the magic we killed had no malice about it. It spat us out, the kids, because we were neither worthy of, nor in need of, its enchantment. If we had not been the selfish, unthinking, destructive beasts that we were, who's to say the magic might not be there yet, under the soil between the two rusty dumpsters, willing, now that we were older, to embrace us as well. To save us, too.

They are young, the lucky handful. Their faces are smooth, their skin is supple, their hair is dark, and though they look right through those of my generation, refusing to acknowledge us, preferring not to admit our existence, their eyes are clear and bright. If you touch them, electricity leaps from their skin. They are alive, vibrantly alive and untouched by the world, for decades now and perhaps forever. And my parents are dead.

I didn't tell Zach any of this, of course.

⟡

We walked through the park. A stiff wind was picking up, swirling fallen leaves across the path, making the heavy branches of the oaks creak and sway.

"You can't despise all children," he said. "Come on, think about it. It's… irrational."

I didn't answer him.

We emerged from the stupid nature trail at a different spot from where we'd entered it. To the left, a picnic area dotted with litter and blankets, directly ahead, a gravel bike path. Not sure where the hell we were, or which direction to head in to find an exit from the park, I paused. A couple of paces behind me, Zach was still nattering on in earnest tones.

More kids. Goddammit. Couldn't catch a break today. Only a couple of yards away ten or twelve of them were sitting in a loose circle around a slightly older girl. The kids were being strangely quiet.

I realized the older girl was telling them a story. Something about her face, her expression, made me look at her twice. Then three times.

Zach said something.

"Shut up," I said.

The girl was kneeling in the grass. She was as thin as a stick, her jawline so sharp it looked as if the bone were about to break through her skin. Her long hair was loose and tangled; she kept pushing it back from her eyes. Her arms were crisscrossed with scratches and dotted with raw bug bites, and her face streaked with dirt. But it was her eyes that held me.

"The bad little boy," she said, "finally got so bad that he wouldn't listen to his mother at all. One time she told him to turn off the TV and go to bed. 'No,' he said. 'You can't tell me what to do. I'm going to do what I want.' And when his mom tried to take the remote, he put up his hand, like this," the girl lifted her right hand; it was filthy, the nails ragged, the knuckles crusty with grime. She closed it into a tight fist. "And he hit his mom, hit her right in the stomach."

She swept her gaze across the faces of her silent audience. "A little while later, the boy got sick. His mom took him to the doctor, but the doctor couldn't do anything. The boy just got sicker. His mom took him to the hospital, but the hospital people said, 'Take him home, we can't help him.' So she took him home. And the little boy got sicker and sicker, and then he died." The girl paused.

The children stared at her, wide-eyed, mouths open. Just behind me, I could feel Zach, holding himself still. His breath was warm on my shoulder. I didn't turn to see what expression he wore. I was more interested in the girl, her grief-struck face, the thread of desperation weaving through her words.

I'd heard this story before. An older version.

"So they buried him," she said. "They put him in a coffin and dug a hole and put him in the hole and covered him over with dirt. And the next day everybody came running to his mom and told her she had to go to the cemetery right away. And when she got there, she saw the little boy's hand sticking out of the grave. His right hand. The one he hit her with." The girl paused again, licked dry lips. "So they dug him up and put his hand back in the coffin, and buried him again. But the next day, his hand was sticking out of the grave again. So everybody ran back to his mom. 'What do you want me to do?' she asked. 'He was a bad boy. He was always bad.' This happened a lot. The people buried the boy over and over, but the next day his hand would always be sticking out of the grave." The girl swallowed. She placed her hands on her knees and leaned forward slightly. "Finally the mother went and got a big stick, and she went to the cemetery and beat the boy's hand black and blue and all bloody. She beat it and beat it and beat it. And then at last the boy pulled his hand back into the grave, and he had peace." The girl stood up. She looked at the kids again, just one brief, sweeping glance, and then she walked off, walked through the circle, walked away into the trees.

Behind me, Zach made a soft sound.

The children looked stunned. The circle began to break apart. A couple of the kids seemed about to cry.

"OK, you were right," I said quietly. "I don't despise all children. That girl right there? If my daughter—"

"Wait," Zach said. "No. She was horrible. She was vile."

"She was magnificent." I turned, then, and caught him with his own hand raised, to touch my arm, touch my shoulder. To touch me. "If a daughter of mine could be just like that, then just maybe I wouldn't mind having one."

I stared into his eyes, absorbing his dismay, his disgust. Then I laughed, and walked away, in search of the exit.

❦

Mister

"Mister? Hey, mister, help me out a minute?"

Reda wasn't a mister, but she turned around anyway. Reda always turned around. There were some men on the street; a couple of them glanced at the kid, but kept walking. Most people in the city kept walking when a stranger called out. Spare some food? Spare some change? Those who walked had nothing to spare. Those who had something to spare never walked.

The girl was one of those who had decided to go, Reda saw immediately. Young for it, she thought. It was easy enough to receive emancipated youth status; fourteen-year-olds got their cards these days by filling out a form any first-year at a legal-aid clinic could walk them through. But this kid didn't look like she'd even hit twelve.

"What do you need help with?" Reda asked.

"Spelling," the girl said. She held up a marker with a gold-colored cap, its expensive brand name clear on the barrel. It was the sort you used when you wanted to draw something that wouldn't wash off. Rich kids who couldn't get their parents to sign off on a permission-to-tattoo slip bought them, but this was no rich kid, not with that complexion, not with those teeth. This one had probably never seen a dentist in her life, or a doctor. A nurse-practitioner working out of a van, at best, and that only if the girl went to school regularly.

"I spell pretty good," Reda said.

"How about punctuation?"

Reda couldn't help staring at the kid's gear. "Looks like you've got everything ready." Boots, canteens, rucksack, all new-looking, all expensive, just like the marker. A wealthy friend? Reda wondered. They presented themselves as friends, didn't they, the ones who went around sniffing after poor kids to sponsor. She hoped not; she hoped the girl had come to her decision by herself. But it had to be difficult to steal items such as these, though she supposed any security system could be out-maneuvered. The kid might even have earned the money to purchase her supplies, though it would have taken a lot of time, with street-level, alley-level, parking-lot-level work. She wouldn't ask; it was none of her business. She did ask, "Which way are you heading?"

"North."

"That's the worst."

"I know it."

The bravery of these children, for it was nearly always children who went, sometimes caused Reda to lie awake at night. She knew that she would never go herself. The gray-black emptiness that surrounded the five or six remaining cities was too vast, too terrifying. You'd need to have the courage of a child to trek out into that, for a child's courage was not that of someone who had nothing to lose, but that of someone who didn't know what they had to lose. It was these children who kept the cities alive, who set out signal beacons for planes, who maintained lighthouses, who kept the roads navigable for the trucks that transported food and goods. The municipal authorities encouraged the citizenry to take excursions to the tops of the city walls, to see the lights glowing and flickering in the gray-black emptiness. Reda had gone once. The other people with her that night had applauded; some had prayed and offered blessings. Reda had kept silent, pushing down her grief and shame. The lights were so tiny, so sparse.

"Have you got food in that rucksack?" she said. "Do you need anything?"

"I need to write a message. And you didn't answer my question."

So cool, this child. So self-possessed and sure of herself. So small, and so thin, and so terribly determined. The municipal authorities made a big show of rewarding out-trekkers who returned—medals, features in the newssheets, a bed in the Hostel of Heroes, food chits. Scholarships to the civil service academy, even, for a few. But not many came back, and of those who did, the majority set out again, with more beacons, more lights, more glow-globes and more thick, black-tipped matches to set the gray grass that flourished in the gray-black emptiness on fire. Any light, even that of the smoky burn of grass fires, was better than no light.

"About punctuation?"

"Yah." The girl looked away for a second. "I want to get it right. It's important."

"Where do you want to use that marker?"

"On me. On my front, and on my back."

"You're going to need someone to do that for you. Especially your back."

"I know it. But only if that person can spell. And knows where the commas go."

"I have to ask you something," Reda said. "Why did you call out for a man? You want someone to write on your body, so…"

"Man, woman, what's the difference? I wasn't talking to you, anyway. I was talking to that guy with the stupid hat."

"Why?"

"He looked old enough, like he could've gone to school back in the before-days."

"I can write," Reda said. "I got my ninth-grade certificate."

"In the before-days?"

"No," she admitted. "I was born after that time."

"Yah, that's what I thought." The girl glanced around. Checking to see if there were any oldsters on the street, probably.

"I'll go away, if you want. If I'm bothering you."

"Nah. You're okay. 'Cept that you look sad."

"Sorry about that." Reda didn't try to put on a smile. It would have been the same as lying. "I can't help it."

The girl nodded. "So you know about commas, or what?"

"I think so," Reda said. "What do you want written?"

"'If you see me, say hi.'"

"If you see me, say hi," Reda repeated.

"On my front, and on my back. I want it to be right, understand? Correct. So do I need a comma?"

Reda thought for a moment. "Yes, you gotta have a comma, after me. And a period after the hi. Unless you want an exclamation point?"

"Nah. But a period, yah, you're right, there's gotta be a period at the end. You sure about the comma?"

"Yes."

"Okay. You know how to use this?" The girl held out the marker.

"Like a pen?"

"Right, but you don't need to push hard."

"I got you."

"Okay." The girl handed her the marker. Reda turned it over a couple of times. It was heavier than it looked. "You slide the cap off with your thumb," the girl said. "You see where?"

"Yes."

"Let's do it." The girl was wearing a loose-necked, rough-weave top, clean-looking but cheap. Market-stall goods. She pulled it over her head and dropped it on the rucksack. She wasn't wearing anything under it. Her chest was still that of a child's. Reda could see every rib. "Front first. Start here." She tapped a spot just under the left knob of her collarbone.

If you see me, say hi. Reda wrote very carefully, each letter separate and neat. She put in the comma. She put in the period.

The girl gazed down, then nodded. "Now my back." She turned around.

Reda wrote the words again, again with neatness and care.

"Thanks," the girl said.

"You don't want me to put your name?"

"Nah. That's fine." She picked up her top, but didn't put it back on. Giving the ink chance to sink in, to bond with the cells of her skin, Reda figured. She capped the marker.

"Who's the message for?" she asked.

"Anybody. Everybody."

She was going to trek about in the gray-black emptiness with her shirt off? *If you see me, say hi.* The courage of children. The ignorant hopefulness of children. She might not encounter a living soul out there. The region to the north was the darkest and the emptiest. Lights set out there died quickly.

The girl put her top back on. Reda returned the marker. "Thank you," she said. "Thank you, and all the others who go out to set lights."

"Somebody's got to, yah?" The girl picked up her canteens and clipped them to the loops of her belt, then slung the rucksack on. "'Bye," she said, and started walking north.

'Bye, Reda began to reply, but in her mouth, the word changed. "Hi," she said, softly. "Hi," she murmured, over and over, until distance and the curve of the street took the bold, brave, striding child out of Reda's view. It didn't help; that night she lay awake again, and cried.

✣

Happyfacing

THAT SATURDAY SHE WAS AFRAID TO LEAVE THE APARTMENT, since she'd been pissing spiders. There was an omen for you, if you believed in omens. She did not, but still. Streams of pinkie-nail-sized buggers, eggshell and dove-gray, racing around and around the bowl. A person could be excused for thinking that might mean something. Besides, the last time she'd ventured outside, there'd been so many blue eyes. Face after face, set with sparkling blue eyes and china-white teeth. Gave her the willies.

But then, so many things did, these days.

Just before noon, someone knocked on the door. She could have yelled at the tap-tap-tapper to go away. But a lady did not raise her voice. She would have to open the door to tell whoever it was to fuck off.

Probably not a neighbor. They knew better than to bother her. There were only a handful of people left in the building, stubborn holdouts like her, clinging on by their teeth and toenails. She was surprised the old coot on the fourth floor was still able to manage the stairs.

Could be whoever was knocking was an itinerant merchant. Maybe even with something useful to sell or trade. Batteries. Dried meat. Wooden matches. Mothballs.

Powdered milk, she thought. It would be wonderful to have a bit of powdered milk. She had enough oatmeal, double-wrapped against vermin and sealed in plastic tubs, to last her for damn near ever, but it just wasn't the same without milk. Or raisins. But raisins were too much to hope for.

The peephole hadn't worked for eleven years. One day the glass had gone cloudy, as if a cataract had grown over it. Even glass got tired. She put her ear to the wood and listened, but could hear no breathing on the other side.

Some people could hold their breath for a long time, and Rippy, just before he disappeared for good, had gotten to the point where he had needed to breathe only once or twice an hour, but still. She lived too close to Blue Street to take stupid risks. The last time she'd seen Rippy, he'd knocked on the door just like this, one-two-three, and then waited. When she opened up, he said he'd come to talk to her cats. You picked a fine time to lose your mind, she'd told him. She'd never owned a cat in her life. She'd kept finches once, a breeding pair pushed on her as a gift by a co-worker in the days when people still went to offices and stores and factories, and collected paychecks. The birds had died inside a month. Naturally she still had the cage. She never threw anything away. Rippy had talked to the empty cage for a few minutes, then run out before she finished boiling water for tea. *You picked a fine time to lose your mind.* Those had been the last words she'd ever spoken to him. She still regretted that.

There was nobody on the other side of the door. But there had been. Though the rest of her was falling apart, her hearing hadn't failed yet.

Falling apart. Falling to bits. Been falling for years, and years. Still hadn't hit the ground. She had to admit to herself that the journey had become more than a little tedious. Nowadays, everything she used to do to smooth the passage had stopped working. Relief came intermittently, more by chance than design, and never lasted more than a few minutes.

Before, people had laughed at her for being a hoarder. Shook their heads when they thought she couldn't see. Clucked their tongues and sighed when they thought she couldn't hear. But she still had coffee, and aspirin, and vitamins, even now. Doled out, rationed, one-a-days becoming once-a-weeks, aspirin only on special occasions, coffee to commemorate some great, fleeting victory against entropy. But still. If she'd been younger, stronger, more of a wheeler-dealer, she might have done well for herself, peddling and trading. But she hadn't had the energy for it. She lacked the necessary patience, and the smooth tongue. But still. She did well enough. Sometimes, when she felt strong, she dropped by the market place in the parking lot of the stripped strip mall. Some folks still accepted gold as a medium of exchange, and her brother had collected coins for years before the collapse. She'd salvaged them after he died. They'd both lived alone, and had entrusted each other with the keys to their apartments. He would have done the same, if she had been the first one to go. They couldn't stand each other, but when the crunch came, they'd sat in the dark and held hands, and come to an unspoken agreement.

Getting old was gutting, even in the best of times. And these were not the best of times.

Day after day, she felt like pounded shit. That never changed. Her left ring finger twitched constantly. She coughed brown. Saw through a shimmer, like desert haze. She got dizzy if she sat too long. Sick to her stomach if she moved too fast. But if she lay in bed all day, her back knotted. Icicles stabbed her hips. When she was a child, she and her brother had played with icicles, holding the fat end in mittened hands, pressing the pointed bits against each other's wrists, inoculating each other against winter.

There was no vaccine for what sickened her now. When the warehouses had burned, how many different toxins had been released into the air, the water, the soil? Thousands. Tens of thousands. That was the real border between the old times and the new. A line etched in time. No going back, except, sometimes, in dreams.

She was accustomed to caring for herself. She was used to people being useless.

That Saturday, she was afraid to go outside. But if she did not, then the next day she would be more afraid. And if she did not go out on Sunday, by Monday she would be cowering under the covers, all her elderly sheets, the quilt she'd stolen after its previous owner had jumped from the roof and which still smelled of cigarettes, the fleece throws she'd gotten cheap at the parking-lot market because their colors were so garish. Huddle and weep, and tremble at the thought of even touching the doorknob. No. She would not step on that path. The way back from it was too long for her now. She was too old. She'd never make it. And there was no one to help her.

There was a certain relief in that, in knowing that nobody would help you. One less thing to hope for. Hopes were so heavy; she'd been glad to lay that particular one down, and kick dirt over it.

So she got dressed. Brushed her teeth with the ancient brush and the trickle of water that still came from the tap. The city was dead, but it wouldn't lie down and be still. Occasionally the electricity even came back on for an hour or two. She wondered how many people it took to accomplish that, and what in the world those folks did to keep themselves from giving up. Cheerleading squads in the power plant, prayer circles around the generators. There was no point in combing her hair. Anything she tried only made it look worse. Outside, she always wore a cap. Which fooled nobody, but still. She'd always frightened people. When she was younger, she'd taken a certain glee in that. Boo! It's the scary lady. When had that started to become tiresome? Long ago. Before the end of the city.

The only reason she'd gone back for Rippy was that he hadn't been afraid of her the first time they met. She'd been working as a messenger. The package hadn't been for him. But he'd looked her in the eyes, smiled, pointed her to the right address. So casually calm, so nonchalantly polite. So when everything crashed, she made her way to where he was and said, Come with me. I know a safer place than this.

She had saved his life that day, but the man never could sit still. Wouldn't stay where it was safe. Wouldn't hunker down to survive.

He had big hands. Always chapped. Always rough-looking. She'd wanted to ask him if they hurt. She'd wanted to offer some lotion. Never gotten around to it. Never had plucked up the courage.

He had been the last person to ever wish her a happy birthday. After he vanished, she'd stopped numbering her years.

All right, now.

Look in the mirror. Smile. Outside required happyfacing. Not for others. Screw other people. She did it for herself.

If she didn't leave the apartment today, she might never leave it again.

Calmly, reasonably, she talked herself into courage.

Outside, though, her vision swam. Her heart raced. She listed to the left. *I can't make it, I can't make it.* But if she turned back, the defeat would finish her.

Courage was a fine thing. A necessary thing. But she was falling, and courage was no parachute.

The sky was yellow. She could still see yellow the best, through the circles of gray. White, gray, and yellow. Yellow used to be her favorite color.

Perhaps the spiders had been an omen, after all.

She had to sit down on the steps of the building. Her fingers twitched. Her face poured sweat. The rest of her was dry. Her mouth, driest of all. No spit to speak of. To speak with. Glass splintered in her back. The hairs in her nostrils burned. She sneezed ash, and her shoulders cracked.

All courage fled. But still. Assume a virtue if you have it not. Oh, that boy had been such a prick to his mother. The girl had been a fool, wasting her sympathy on him.

She was not sorry she'd gone outside. Better to land here, than on her kitchen floor. She remembered holding her brother's hand. They'd hated each other. But in the end, all hands were the same.

She managed to get the keys out of her pocket and lay them on the step beside her.

Who had been knocking on her door? There had been no footprints in the hall, no human smell lingering in the still air.

There were humans on the street. She could hear them. Boots and flip-flops, stealthy edgings and dragging gaits, a few confident clops. Humans. And others. But still. They were all in the same mess together, above Blue Street and below, in the dead city and the dying world.

Spiders trickled, tickling, down her legs.

Spitless, she cleared her throat. Once there had been a woman named Judy. Rippy had loved her. He'd never said it; she'd read the devotion in his eyes. When he lost her, more than his heart had broken. She had thought, once, that they might have comforted each other. But she had been too beaten down to reach up, and he had gone numb to words.

She put on the biggest smile she could. Happyfacing. Not important, except to her. But still. Go out the way you came in. Her mother had told her how she'd laughed as a baby, laughed so loudly that strangers on the street turned to look, and couldn't help but grin themselves. Not that she could remember what had been so funny, but still.

"People," she called. The breath she took drew sand into her lungs, gray grains, spiked and jagged. "Everybody. Go to my place and take something. Spring cleaning."

She was used to people being useless. In the end, this did not absolve her. One more strike against entropy. The last one. It did not make her a good person, but still. Would she have taken them all with her if she could? No. They all had a right to fall at their own pace.

You lived with regrets; died with them, too. They were not as heavy as hopes, but still. Burdens.

She missed aspartame, and the internet.

It couldn't have been Rippy, knocking at the door. Though it had sounded exactly like him. He had trudged down into the heart of the triangle below Blue Street, and never returned. She regretted, now, that she hadn't been able to scratch up the courage to touch him, not even once. Nothing would have changed. But still. It took courage to lay that regret down. In the end, she didn't have enough.

She had stopped breathing before the first scavenger snatched up her keys.

GRANDPA LOST HIS TOOTHBRUSH

GRANDPA LOST HIS TOOTHBRUSH, SO HE WAS IN THE bathroom squeezing toothpaste on his finger. He always leaves the door open, no matter what he's doing in there. This drives Aunt Marcellina crazy.

Lots of things drive Aunt Marcellina crazy. She hates that Grandpa smokes, so a long time ago she threw away all the ashtrays. Now he uses any cup or saucer or plate that's handy, and if there aren't any handy, he lets the ashes drop on the floor. Grinds the cigarettes out on the floor, too. When he's wearing shoes. Sometimes even when he's not. They fight about this every day.

Aunt Marcellina drives Grandpa crazy, too. She makes us eat oatmeal for breakfast, and Grandpa can't stand the stuff. So whenever Aunt Marcellina sets a bowl of it in front of him, he stands up and dumps the glop in the trash. Then she turns purple and screams at him for wasting food. Then he says some bad words and she yells at him for that.

"Why do you let her live with you?" I asked, soon after I came to live with Grandpa, too.

"Family is family," he said. "You can't turn your back on family. Well, you can, but then you'd be a goddamned son of a bitch. Marcellina knows she's got a home here for as long as she lives. You, too, kid."

Aunt Marcellina is not my aunt. She's Grandpa's aunt. She's not older than him, though. She's Grandpa's father's youngest sister, or something like that. She used to have a job and an apartment. She used to live in another city. One day she came to visit Grandpa and his wife—my Grandma, but I never met her—and she never left. Grandpa and Grandma had kids. Aunt Marcellina stayed. Grandma died. Aunt Marcellina stayed. All the kids grew up and left. Aunt Marcellina stayed.

This is not my home. I'm not staying here a minute longer than I have to. The only reason I'm related to these people is because nine months before I was born, a condom broke. My mom said that to me once. Her exact words were, "The only reason you're here is because that goddamn condom broke." I was four years old when she said that, but I remember. That was before she disappeared, and a long time before I knew Grandpa and Aunt Marcellina even existed.

Grandpa didn't really lose his toothbrush. He threw it at Aunt Marcellina when she was yelling at him for leaving the bathroom door open. She was standing in the hall, and he spun around and hurled it right at her head. Aunt Marcellina dodged, so it hit the wall. She picked it up with her finger and thumb, like it was a dead mouse, and threw it in the garbage.

"Grandpa?"

"What?" he said, without turning around. He was squeezing out a long stripe of toothpaste on his finger.

"Aunt Marcellina went out."

"Good."

"Grandpa."

"What?"

"I'm bored."

"Jesus Christ, kid, go play or something."

He hadn't gotten dressed today. Not dressed to go out. He was wearing ratty old pajama bottoms and a t-shirt that was more holes than shirt. The veins in his feet were blue. His toenails were yellow. Aunt Marcellina hated it when Grandpa didn't get dressed. She told him it wasn't decent. Then he'd yell that it was his house, goddammit, and he'd sit around butt naked if he wanted to.

"Grandpa."

"Mother of god. Don't you have any homework to do?"

"It's Saturday, Grandpa."

He grunted. "What time is it?"

"Around one."

"So she won't be back for a couple of hours."

Aunt Marcellina always had lunch with her friends Mrs. Waller and Mrs. Tepecik on Saturday, and then she did some shopping. Aunt Marcellina liked routines. Monday to Friday, she went out in the mornings. That didn't help me any, since I was in school. She was always home when I got back. I never got a break from her, except on Saturdays.

"Grandpa, can I have a cat?"

Grandpa stuck his finger in his mouth and started spreading toothpaste over the five or six teeth he still had in there. This was a little disgusting. He ran the water, bent his head to take a swig and swish it all around. He spit. He spit again. Whenever I complained about anything, Aunt Marcellina would tell me I was very lucky indeed to live in a house with running water AND electricity. Not a lot of people were as fortunate as me. He took another gulp of water and swished some more. After he spat that out, he said, "Don't be a dumbshit. You know how she feels about cats."

I knew. The thing about Aunt Marcellina that drove Grandpa the craziest was how she always rushed out to the yard, front or back, it didn't matter, and hexed any cat that set foot on the property. Loudly. In full view of the neighbors. Grandpa always had to run and haul her back inside. He told her that one fine day she'd look out the window and see the whole goddamned neighborhood out there with pitchforks and torches and a stake to roast her on, and god save him if he knew why they hadn't done it yet, and when that happened she'd have no cause for any bitching, because she'd been asking for it for a long time.

In the foster home with Mrs. San, they'd had a cat. It was nice. It was the nicest thing in that place. We had electricity for three hours a day, but we had to get our water from the government truck. Mrs. San made us eat oatmeal, too, and she never did the laundry so the kids at school made fun of me because I smelled. So I tried to wash some of my clothes in the bathtub, and Mrs. San found me and started hitting me with the toilet brush. We were only allowed to flush the toilet after we did number two, and then we had to scrub the bowl. There were four kids living there then. Two of them were older than me, so they made me scrub the toilet when it was their turns. The other one was just a baby.

"Grandpa?"

"What the hell is it now?"

"Will you tell me a story?"

He didn't turn around. He looked at me in the mirror above the sink. His eyes were droopy, and he hadn't shaved for a few days, so his face was covered with white bristles. Grandpa hated shaving. He would've grown a beard a long time ago, but Aunt Marcellina wouldn't let him. "You know how to make coffee?"

"Yes." I did. I used to do it at the second group home I was in. The first group home, I was only there for a couple of days. I don't remember it too well. But I lived in the second one for almost a year. I don't want to say the name of the couple who ran it. I don't want to remember that place. But making coffee was one of my jobs.

"Scoot yourself into the kitchen and get a pot started. I gotta take a dump."

"Okay," I said, and by the time he got to the kitchen I had the coffee ready and a cup and saucer and spoon and sugar on the table (Grandpa never put milk in his coffee), and an extra saucer for him to use as an ashtray. When I came to live at Grandpa's house, Aunt Marcellina sighed and said, "Now we're going to have to budget for milk." Then she said that if he'd give up his blasted cigarettes, they could afford chicken once in a while. He said, "Those no-winged, stump-legged things they call chickens now? No thanks."

"Christ." He looked at the table, then looked at me. He scratched his chest through one of the holes in his t-shirt.

"I miss television, I really do. So what kind of story do you want, kid?"

"Tell me a story about Blue Street."

He snorted. "You like monster stories now? I'd have thought you had enough nightmares already."

"It doesn't have to be a monster story."

"You scream the house down, and then blab to Marcellina, she'll skin me alive." He filled his cup, dumped a ton of sugar in it, and sipped it without even stirring it. Then he got his cigarettes from the top of the refrigerator. He lit one. Then he sat down.

Then I sat down.

Grandpa finished his coffee and poured some more. He finished his cigarette, and lit another one.

"Once upon a time," he said.

"Not that way."

"What way do you want?"

"The real way."

"Jesus." He closed his eyes. "Ribbie lived in a little green house made of old oil drums and spackle, and he was famous for his sorrows." Grandpa lifted one droopy eyelid. "Okay?"

"Is this going to be sad?"

"No, the sorrows are a different story. But he was famous for them, so I just thought I'd mention that."

"Okay."

"Ribbie was a trader and a peddler, making his living by buying and selling. He traveled up and down and right and left, carrying his goods on his back, or pulling them along behind him on a wagon he'd made himself out of an old crate and some wheels he pried off a baby carriage. Everybody knew him. He was a sharp dealer, but not a crook. And because he was famous for his sorrows, he was popular at funerals. He had a real knack for getting the mourning going good."

"Did he have a cat?"

"He didn't even have a goldfish. Now, this Ribbie didn't trade below Blue Street. He was kind of a nervous sort, and people liked to scare him, you know, tell him stories about creatures in the sewers and flying rat-people constructing their own city on the roofs of abandoned buildings."

"I thought you said he was popular and stuff."

"So?"

"So why did they want to scare him?"

"Because people are shits. Now, Ribbie bought and sold, and traded and bartered, but he also collected. And there came a time when he had walked up and down and right and left and all over what remained of the world, and nowhere could he find what he wanted. So he put all his best trade goods in his backpack, and all his traveling gear in his wagon, and all his courage in his pocket, and set out for Blue Street.

"Now, getting across Blue Street wasn't hard. The road and sidewalks were all broken up and his wagon bumped and jumped, and he stubbed his toe on a chunk of concrete, but that was it. Nothing jumped out of the shadows to eat him up. Nobody swooped down from the rooftops to tear his throat out. In fact, there weren't any rooftops, because that whole block had been leveled. Flat, you understand? It was pretty much a no-man's-land."

"The monsters lived further in."

"No monsters. Didn't you say there didn't have to be monsters? So. Okay. It was a fine spring day and the sun was shining. Ribbie started to whistle, and some birds whistled back. He kept on whistling, until suddenly he realized what he thought were birds whistling back at him weren't birds at all, but a man with a hairy, snouty face and long nails like claws who was sitting on a pile of broken bricks and crap like that, and another man with spiky white hair and no pants on who was standing next to the pile of broken bricks. They smiled and waved. Ribbie considered running away, but he had his courage in his pocket, so he patted it three times for luck, and trudged on."

"Who were the weird guys?"

"They were the Border Patrol. 'Welcome, friend,' said the hairy-faced man. 'What's your business here?'

"Ribbie said, 'I'm a traveler and a trader, a dealer and a wheeler. I buy and I sell, I barter and I swap. I thought I'd try my luck in your fair town.'

"And Mr. No-pants said, 'Town? We are an independent republic, you asshole.' It was like he wanted to start a fight. Ribbie felt the spit dry up in his mouth. But the other guy patted Mr. No-pants on the shoulder, and said, 'Free enterprise is good for business.'"

"Grandpa, now you're just making stuff up."

"Kid, you said you wanted a story. Stories are made up."

"I want a real story."

"Stick with me, okay? This is a real story."

"You promise?"

"You have my goddamn word." He lit another cigarette. "So the hairy guy, he asks Ribbie what he's got to sell. So Ribbie, what can he do? He takes off his pack and lays out some of his wares. Mechanical pencils with extra leads. Eyeglasses. Freeze-dried chewing gum. You ever have that? It's nasty. A busted flashlight. Some plastic bags in pretty good shape. An ink-jet printer cartridge, vacuum-sealed. Buttons. Hand-made fly-swatters. You know. The usual.

"And the hairy guy starts laughing. He slaps Mr. No-pants on the back, and says, 'What do you think, Bill?' Mr. No-pants starts laughing, too. 'Friend,' says the hairy guy, 'you are going to get your ass handed to you if you go to the market lot with this junk. I wouldn't trade my mother for your whole pack.'

"Ribbie's eyes get real wide. 'Really?' he says. 'What would you trade her for?' And the Border Patrol stops laughing, just like *that*." Grandpa snapped his fingers.

"Mr. No-pants showed his teeth. Before, he was laughing with his head turned away, so Ribbie couldn't see. Now, he wanted him to see. His mouth was crammed with maybe a hundred teeth, tiny, slender, and pointed, like a fish's. Only his were red. The hairy guy bent his fingers, to show his nails. He could push them out and pull them back, like a cat. Now don't you start in about cats again."

I didn't.

"Now, Ribbie began worrying he might be in trouble, and he hadn't even crossed the border yet. But remember he had his courage with him, and besides, he'd walked the world, or what was left of it, and this wasn't the first time people had showed their teeth, or their claws. Or their guns or their machetes or their socks full of rocks. He put on his best peddler's smile, and said, 'I'm not joking. I'm a serious businessman, me. What would you sell your mother for?'

"Hairy face said, 'Believe me, you wouldn't want her.' And Mr. No-pants said, 'Hey, she's not as bad as mine.'

"Our Ribbie here, he kept on smiling. He took some more items out of his pack. Pipe tobacco. Ear plugs. Fishing line. A can of vanilla frosting. Eucalyptus cough drops. A ten-hole harmonica. A couple of magazines. A peg-board chess set. All of a sudden, the Border Patrol looked hungry. And Ribbie said, 'I'll take my chances at this market lot you mentioned. If you would be so kind as to direct me there?' He talked like that to show he wasn't a dumbshit.

"Mr. No-pants said, 'So what is it you're looking to buy?'

"Ribbie figured he had them, then. 'Mothers'll do. This is good stuff here. Worth more than one. You got a mother, too, huh?'

"Mr. No-pants said, 'Yeah,' but the hairy guy broke in. 'We could just kill you here and take your shit, and nobody would ever know.'

"Ribbie felt his courage grow. 'Nobody? Not even all those folks watching from across the street?' Because across the street there were buildings still standing, and the buildings had windows, and at every window he could see three, four, five, six people crowding together, peering out, watching. 'And besides,' he went on, 'if you kill me you can take all this stuff, sure. But that would be your one and only shot at getting your hands on quality goods like these. Back home, I have storehouses crammed to the ceiling with all manner of desirables. We do business now, maybe in a month or two I'd swing around this way again, and we could do business again. Now you think about that. You think about that for a minute,' Ribbie said, getting nervous again, starting to sweat, because the hairy guy with the snout had pushed his claws all the way out and from where he was standing, they looked as long and sharp as a panther's. And the other guy, with the spiky white hair and red fish teeth, he had no pants, remember? But he had something wrapped round and around his waist, and as Ribbie kept talking, doing his patter, this something started twitching and loosening—unwinding. Uncoiling, like a snake, and Ribbie got to worrying he'd come all this way just to end up strangled by some mutant bastard's six-foot dick."

"What about the people watching?"

"Which people watching what, now?"

Grandpa froze with his coffee cup halfway to his lips. I slid off my chair and got set to bolt out the back door, in case she blamed me.

It was Aunt Marcellina, home early from her Saturday afternoon out. There was no door between the kitchen and living room, just a rectangular entryway, where someone could have hung a door if they'd wanted to. I guess Grandpa never wanted to. Aunt Marcellina stood there in the entryway, two shopping bags at her feet, peeling her gloves off. She always wore gloves when she left the house. Except when she ran out to hex the cats.

"Just telling the kid a story," Grandpa muttered.

"Why aren't you dressed yet? It's the middle of the afternoon! And I see you still haven't taken the trouble to shave."

She was mad at him, not me. Grandpa sent me a signal with his eyes. *Get.*

"Is that coffee?"

"No, it's this new kind of mud-colored vodka."

"You won't sleep a wink tonight. Oh, lord." She fanned the air. "You're poisoning all of us with that vile tobacco, and you know it perfectly well. Where do you think you're going?" That was to me.

"Outside? To play?"

"You have chores to do."

"Oh, give the kid a break. It's Saturday."

"The green ants don't take Saturdays off. Now do they? Do they, child?"

"No, ma'am," I said.

So I had to put on my stomping boots and get the bucket and brush and dustpan from under the sink, and go down to the basement and kill green ants. "I want that bucket full, do you hear me?" Aunt Marcellina said. "Not half full. Not three quarters full. Full."

I hate killing the green ants. It's the worst chore ever. They're almost as big as mice used to be in the old days, and they make this awful *squeak* noise when you break them. But they eat plastic, and Aunt Marcellina says it's our duty to humanity to kill as many of them as we can. I don't know why it always has to be my duty, though. Fortunately the stupid green ants are slow and pretty much blind. Not like the blade-birds. Aunt Marcellina won't even let me go to school when there is a blade-bird alert, even though the school here has a special armored bus.

"Can I go out when I'm finished?"

"We'll see," she said, and went back to yelling at Grandpa some more.

And of course that afternoon the green ants decided to play shy. They like water and damp places. Sometimes after it rains, the sidewalks are covered with them, a roiling carpet of green. And Grandpa's house is old and the basement is always damp. It was damp that Saturday, too. Even so, I couldn't find more than twenty or thirty green ants to stomp. I was in the basement for hours. And then Aunt Marcellina came down. She called me lazy and said since I liked to goof off so much, I could stay down there all night and see how I liked that. If I wanted any dinner I'd better fill that bucket at least halfway, and if I planned to sleep in my bed instead of on the gol-darned cement floor, that bucket had better be crammed up to the brim.

She let me come up from the basement to pee, but then I had to go right back down.

After a while, everything got quiet upstairs. No more footsteps. I figured Aunt Marcellina and Grandpa had finished their dinner and gone to bed.

I was tired, too. My bucket still had only about thirty broke-backed and head-stomped green ants in it, but I was about to fall over.

If I turned the lights out, I knew they'd pick that exact moment to come swarming out of the cracks they were hiding in, so I didn't. I didn't like it down there, but I wasn't going to cry or anything. But even Mrs. San never made me stay in a basement all night. A closet, yeah, but never a basement. Though to be fair, that was probably because her house didn't have a basement.

The floor was cold. I had to lie on my stomach to keep the light out of my eyes. I made my arms into a pillow. I'd slept like that plenty of times before. No problem. Only not in a basement. But it was no big deal.

"Kid." I woke up with Grandpa's hard yellow toenails poking my ribs. "Come on, get upstairs and go to bed."

"But Aunt Marcellina—"

"Hell with her. This is still my house, goddammit. No, leave the bucket. Leave everything. Come on." He put his hand on my shoulder and steered me up the stairs and through the hall, and up the other stairs to my bedroom. Then he unlaced my big boots and pulled them off. He told me to never mind my pajamas and just get under the covers.

"Grandpa?"

"Yeah?"

"What happened to Ribbie?"

"Kid, go to sleep. I'll tell you the rest tomorrow."

"But I want to know what happened."

"Shit, kid, it's just a story. You can finish it any way you want. Action. Ribbie pulls out a gun and blasts the ever-loving guts out of all and sundry. Romance. Ribbie finds the love of his life on Blue Street, and they settle down there and live happily ever after. Surprise ending. Ribbie throws off his coat, sprouts wings, and flies off into the morning sky. Or he grows roots and turns into a man-tree. Use your imagination."

"But I want to hear how you finish it."

"Christ almighty." Grandpa sat down on my bed. He sighed. He rubbed his eyes. They looked red, and droopier than ever. Aunt Marcellina was probably right about the coffee keeping him up. "And here I was thinking I'd done my time on the bedtime story brigade. Though to tell you the truth, I wasn't any great shakes at it the first time around. Fact is, I wasn't any great shakes at much. So."

I thought he was going to say something more, so I waited. Grandpa nudged me with his elbow. "What?"

"So where did we leave off?"

"The monsters were going to eat him, and all the people were watching from the windows."

"What monsters? There's no monsters."

"The guy with the fish teeth and the other one with the rat face—"

"I never said rat face. I said hairy, with a snout. Okay, I remember now. The Border Patrol. They saw some of the things old Ribbie carried with him to trade and sell, and their eyes got hungry. Ribbie got a little nervous, sure, but he was a dealer and a wheeler and a glib-tongued son of a bitch, so—"

"But the hairy-faced man had his claws out, and the one with the fish teeth was going to bite him, and his teeth were *red*, like blood—"

"Sure, sure. But Ribbie had been in plenty of tight spots before. Kid, if you have nightmares, I swear I'm never gonna tell you a Blue Street story again."

"I never have nightmares."

"Ri-ight. Well, anyway. So he said, Ribbie said, 'You can take my trade goods, you can slice me and dice me and boil me for dinner, but then you'll never get any more, and I've got shitloads of good stuff back home, I've got storehouses and safehouses and wheelhouses crammed full of all kinds of desirable amenities, and you'll never see a scrap or a thread of them if you mess with me now.'

"So the hairy-faced guy, he thought about that, and he pulled his claws back. His fingers looked almost normal again. And the white-haired guy, he closed his mouth. 'How much for the lot?' asked the hairy guy.

"Ribbie said, 'What do you mean, the lot?'

"'All of it. Your whole load.'

"Now, Ribbie put his hand on his chin and made like he was thinking real hard. He thought so long and hard the Border Patrol started sweating a little themselves, glancing at each other out of the sides of their eyes, you know. Because the more they looked at his trade goods, the hungrier they got. Finally Ribbie nodded, like he'd come to a decision, and said, 'Two mothers. Can't take any less.'

"The white-haired guy—oh, right, he had no pants—"

"And a six-foot dick."

"People always exaggerate. It was four foot, tops. Mr. No-pants burst out, 'Two mothers?'

"And Ribbie jerked his chin at the people all crowded at their windows, and said, 'I bet if I took my merchandise over to your market lot, I could get three or four. Three, four, easy. Listen, you hicks, over at Tunbridge, you can get a mother for half a bolt of homespun and one rusty scissor blade. Independent republic, my ass. You dumbfucks haven't even got your basic running water back yet. And what about electricity? Still with the candles and the floating-wick lamps made out of old soap dishes?'

"Didn't that piss them off?"

"Don't say pissed off. Oh, Ribbie knew what he was doing. Putting them on the defensive, see. Calling them poor, you get it? So then they had to prove they weren't. Like when I tell Marcellina she can't cook beans for shit, so then she makes chili. You follow?"

"I guess. Grandpa?"

"What?"

"Aunt Marcellina says you're scared of the dark. And of getting haircuts. And yellow clouds."

"Marcellina can go take a flying jump. She's one to talk. At least I'm not paranoid about cats. Any case, there's some things you'd be a fool not to be scared of."

"Why does Aunt Marcellina hate cats so much?"

"I'll tell you that story when you're a little older. Anyway. Ribbie's poking their buttons, you follow me? He says, 'Because maybe I'd like to do business with you again, I'm willing to take a loss, this one time. Two mothers, and you get the lot. But you know, I'm a busy man. People to see, places to go. So make up your minds, or give me a pass to the market lot.'

"The Border Patrol wave him away, and they put their heads together and whisper a bit. Then they wave him back, and Mr. No-pants says, 'How about you throw in the stuff in your wagon.'

"Ribbie goes, 'That's my personal traveling gear. Nothing special. Just a tent and some pots, and a sleeping bag, and some tarps, and water purification pills, and pemmican. What do you need that crap for?'

"Hairy guy says, 'The wagon load too, or no deal.'

"So Ribbie goes, 'You gonna play it like that, I need to see these mothers first. I don't want any grandmothers, you know, or spinster second cousins. Don't you be trying to pull a fast one, now.' And the Border Patrol, they look at each other, and the hairy guy gives a little nod. Mr. No-pants nods back, then ambles off, hops over the barricade and into the warren of streets that are still more or less intact.

"Hairy-face says, 'Two genuine mothers, guaranteed. Shit, man, they're mine and Bill's. You're getting a real bargain. Neither one's past sixty. They're good for a lot of years yet. Now get your stuff off the wagon.'

"Ribbie says, 'When I see the goods.'

"So they wait, until No-pants comes back, leading a couple old ladies. The old ladies look plenty pissed off, probably because they're tied together with a length of rope, and one of them is laying into No-pants pretty good with the blade of her tongue, and when the other one catches sight of Hairy-face, she starts in, too."

"So they were really their own mothers?"

"Yep. So Ribbie unloads his wagon, and because he's a nice guy, he tells the old ladies they can sit in the wagon and he'll pull them to their new home. The old ladies say, "Wait until we're clear of the rubble at least, you numbnuts, otherwise you'll shake and rattle our bones to bits," and Ribbie concedes they have a point there. So he takes the rope from No-pants, and grabs the handle of the wagon in his other hand. He can't wave goodbye, but he gives the Border Patrol a nod and a big smile, which neither of them really notices since they've already started squabbling over the flashlight and the vanilla frosting and the paper clips, and he nods at all the spectators pressed against the windows, and when he gets far enough away that he can be sure Hairy-face and No-pants can't hear him, Ribbie laughs and laughs, because of course he got exactly what he wanted." Grandpa patted my knee. "You think you can go to sleep now, kid?"

"But what did Ribbie do with the mothers?"

"Why, he put them with the rest, of course. Didn't I tell you he was a collector?"

"Yeah."

"Well, that's what he collected. Mothers."

"But why?"

"Trying to find a good one. Oh, I think when he started— and Ribbie was only a youngster when he started—he was trying to find the *best* one. But by the time he made his way over what remained of the world and finally down to Blue Street, he'd figured out that a good one was good enough. Good enough for him, you understand? Because everyone's different, and what's good enough for one person isn't exactly right for the next."

"What did he do with the ones that weren't good enough?"

"Oh, he kept them, the ones that wanted to stay. Put them to work, if they wanted to be useful. Let them go, if they wanted. Every year he tried out five, six, seven mothers. More in a good year. You see, the thing about Ribbie was that he was a stubborn bastard. Never gave up. He was disappointed over and over again, naturally, but he kept telling himself that one day he'd find the mother that was good enough for him. So he kept trying." Grandpa reached to turn off the light. "Time to go to sleep now, kid."

"Wait."

"Christ, that's the end of the story. What do you want now, a drink of water?"

"No. Grandpa, that can't be the end of the story. Did Ribbie ever find the mother he wanted?"

"I don't know. All I can tell you is that he never gave up looking." Grandpa stood up, and switched my light off, and left.

The next day I figured Aunt Marcellina would really let me have it, but she didn't say a word to me. I went outside to play right after breakfast, but I didn't really go out to play. I went to look at the homes in the neighborhood. The little ones and the big ones and the middle-sized ones. The wooden ones and the stone ones and the ones made out of oil drums, and the ones made out of crates and tarps. The ones with lots of people inside, and the ones with only one. The ones with kids and the ones without. The ones with mothers and the ones without. I didn't want to get lost, so I kept swinging back toward Grandpa's house to keep my bearings. I saw Aunt Marcellina standing at a window a couple of times, and then I saw her standing at the front door. Grandpa must've been just inside, because she turned and asked, loudly, "Whatever is that child doing?"

I couldn't hear what Grandpa said. Besides, I was pretending not to notice her.

"Playing? That's an odd sort of playing, if you ask me."

And then:

"I'll thank you not to take that tone with me. You're a disgusting old man. You should be ashamed of yourself. No, I won't come inside. You look like a bum, and you smell worse. I don't care if it is your house. There is such a thing as propriety. Wandering around half the night, not letting decent people sleep—"

And then:

"A story? What kind of story?"

I'd edged pretty much out of earshot by then. I didn't catch what she said next.

It was a fine spring day. The sun was shining. Some of the neighbors smiled at me. Some of them narrowed their eyes and wrinkled up their noses. I didn't care. None of the homes I saw were good enough, but that didn't matter. It was only my first day of looking. Grandpa said Ribbie looked for years, and never gave up.

I spied some cats on the steps of an old, broken-down wooden house. I didn't figure anybody lived inside that house. The windows were all busted out and a part of the roof had collapsed. The cats were sitting placidly on the rotten, splintery steps. One was gray, one was black-and-white, and one was mostly white with a little orange. Their front paws all in a row, their tails wrapped neatly around their bodies, they looked like they were waiting. The way cats, especially in groups, always seem to be waiting for something. Serene and patient. As I came closer, the gray cat blinked. The mostly white one with a little bit of orange turned its head slightly. The black-and-white one didn't move at all.

"Hello," I said. I thought, If Aunt Marcellina could see me now, she would kill me. "I have a question, if that's all right." Oh, she would really kill me. She'd kill me dead.

The gray cat and the little-bit-orange one looked at each other. The black-and-white one licked a paw, nonchalantly.

Well, they hadn't said no.

"I'm searching for a good home. A good enough home. To tell you the truth, I only started today. I'm pretty sure that home isn't here, though. Can you tell me where I should look?"

The little-bit-orange cat and the gray cat looked at each other again. Then they looked at me, and shook their heads.

Damn. Then I thought, maybe I asked the question wrong. You have to be careful with this sort of thing.

"Um… will I ever find one?"

"That's two questions," the gray cat said.

"I know. Sorry."

"Yes," said the little-bit-orange one. The gray cat glared at it, but the little-bit-orange one just shrugged.

I couldn't help it. I started grinning, and jumping up and down. I must've looked like an idiot, but I didn't care. They said yes! Well, the little-bit orange cat did, and that was good enough. "One more, one more!"

The gray cat hissed. The little-bit-orange one said, "Oh, play fair. Two will get you three. That's the rule." The gray cat looked disgusted, and twitched its whiskers.

"I need to know where I can get a good toothbrush."

All three cats glared at me.

Oh. Right. "Where can I get a good toothbrush?"

And the black-and-white cat said, "Walk north on this street until you get to the end of the block, then turn left. You will see a yellow house, and a blue house, then some debris, and then two more blue houses. Do not go to the first blue house. Do not go to the second blue house. Go to the third blue house. The man who lives there has got at least a dozen toothbrushes. You'll have to trade him your socks, though."

"Why my socks?"

But three didn't get you four. I knew that. It never had, not since the beginning of time.

"Thank you," I said to the cats. They ignored me, but that was okay.

When I got home, Aunt Marcellina yelled at me for staying out so long. Then she yelled at me because I'd lost my socks. Then she sent me to the basement again to stomp green ants. There were plenty of them this time, so I filled the bucket pretty quick.

When I came upstairs, Grandpa was in the kitchen, smoking. Aunt Marcellina was in her room, doing something. It involved banging. Maybe she was trying to fix her dresser drawers again.

"Grandpa."

He rolled his eyes. "What."

"I have a present for you."

"Don't need anything."

"That's okay," I said. "I want you to have it anyway." I slid the toothbrush across the table. He put his cigarette down on a rusty old jar lid he was using for an ashtray. I guess Aunt Marcellina had pitched a fit about messing up the saucers again. Grandpa raised his eyebrows.

"Don't go thinking this means I gotta tell you stories every night."

"No. Just when you feel like it."

"Kid, I don't feel like it very often."

"That's okay."

We heard Aunt Marcellina coming down the stairs. Grandpa made the toothbrush disappear up his sleeve. He winked at me. I nodded. When Aunt Marcellina appeared in the entryway of the kitchen, she immediately yelled at me to go and wash.

"Yes, ma'am."

She gave me a funny look. I knew it was because I was smiling. Grandpa was smiling, too. Aunt Marcellina didn't know what to make of the pair of us. "I don't know what to make of the pair of you," she said. Grandpa started laughing, but I was already out of the kitchen by then, so I didn't get to see Aunt Marcellina's expression. I heard her yelling, though, even after I had shut the bathroom door. I didn't care. She could yell all she wanted. I didn't stop smiling, and Grandpa didn't stop laughing, either.

Tomorrow, after school, I'd look again. And the next day. And the next. For years, if I had to. Cats didn't lie. Everybody knew that. If I was stubborn like Ribbie, and never quit trying, I would find what I wanted. Not even ten

Aunt Marcellinas could change that. I washed my hands. I washed my face. I brushed my teeth, just for the hell of it. Then I started to whistle.

Two seconds later, Aunt Marcellina started yelling. She must've been standing at the bottom of the steps. Must've run there. She could move real fast for an old lady. Her voice came through the bathroom door loud and clear. What did I think I was doing, making such a racket?

I didn't answer her. I just kept whistling.

The Old Husband's Tale

CLEANING THE REFRIGERATOR WAS SUPPOSED TO BE HIS job, but he couldn't bring himself to care any more. Wilted carrots, expired yogurt, the jar with only two ancient olives left in it, floating forlornly in the brine… so what. Just so what. He let the recycling go, too, allowing the newspapers to pile up, tossing bottles and cans into the regular trash. She, however, carried on with her chores, cooking, dusting, making the bed, as if nothing had happened. He watched her, a scout keeping an eye on the enemy's movements. Her coolness chilled him. Wiping a cloth over the bookshelves, she hummed. Smoothing the sheets, she sang to herself. She'd always done that. But now the melodies were different, the words esoteric. Rhymes and chants. Cantrips, workings. Why not. The secret was out. He put his hands over his ears, but the rhythms soaked into his skin.

He no longer drank the nightcap she fixed for him. Meeting her eyes (be bold, be bold!) he poured it into the sink. His chin quivered; she smiled tightly, and the next night prepared a fresh drink.

They still slept in the same bed, but did not touch. Often, when he woke in the night, she was gone. Sometimes he opened his eyes, and she was lying there next to him, snoring lightly, that same snore he had first heard on their honeymoon, the same soft rasp as she inhaled, that almost-whistle in the back of her nose, the same, the same, and then he would miss her fiercely, with a longing that constricted his heart.

Most nights, she slipped from their bed and opened the window wide. How had he not wakened for so many years, drink or no drink? I was working then, he thought, always exhausted, all the overtime, so many Saturdays,

Sundays, holidays eaten up. He'd been short-tempered with the kids, keep it down, go to your rooms, stop making so much noise. They'd been afraid of him, they said now. To his face, they said it. Afraid of him, the one who paid for their straight teeth and their cars and their diplomas, their first marriages and their divorces. He couldn't believe it. Not afraid of her, who took off her nightgown in the dark of the moon, who rubbed flowers over her skin until the petals turned to curls of ash, who shrank and stretched and became whippet, gray and lean, became cat, smooth-muscled and bristly, became hare, so squat and furtive, and bounded out into the night. The kids called two or three times a week. If he answered the phone, all he got was: Hi Dad, is Mom there? Flat, dismissive.

The kids. Grown women now. How long had they known? Maybe forever, he thought. From childhood. Perhaps they were the same. Perhaps she had taught them the flower-petal trick, the ointment dance, the rhymes and the tunes, the stretching of skin and compressing of bone; perhaps his daughters, too, changed their shapes and flew out of their bedrooms, abandoning oblivious husbands and lovers, became owls or eagle, foxes or muskrats, does of deer and does of rabbits.

When she returned, cold from the night air, flushed from the flight, he would lie as a corpse, his eyes closed and breathing stilled. He had seen. He had no need to see it again, the putting back on of her shape. But sometimes, like today, if he dozed off once more, even for a few moments, when he woke, blinking in the light, for a heartbeat, or two, or ten, he would not remember, and lay his hand on her arm, or on her soft hip. Today, it had happened again. At once she rose, without a word or a glance, shedding his touch with a shiver. That he could forget shocked him. That she shunned him made him furious. He hadn't done anything wrong. He had merely opened his eyes and seen what she would not have had him see. And so she stalked from the room as if disgusted by his presence. How did he deserve that? It wasn't fair.

For an hour he lay in their bed alone, his mouth full of salt. When he got up, he went into the kitchen. She was cleaning out the refrigerator. A roll of paper towels and a spray bottle of the orange cleaner he detested sat on top of the old, grumbling machine. A black trash bag, a quarter full, slumped next to the refrigerator, and the two bottom crisper drawers sat on the kitchen floor. He didn't see her at first, and thought she must have stepped out, gone to the bathroom or outside to the garden for a moment, for the refrigerator door, wide open, blocked his view; cold air swirled around his ankles. He took a step, and another, and there she was, sitting on the kitchen floor as well, holding an apple in her hand.

She gazed at the apple with love. It was a rather small one, and a rather old one, the reddish-yellow skin wrinkled, withered. She smiled at it with tenderness, her eyes misty. It was one of those fancy kinds he couldn't keep straight in his mind, Gala or Roma or Maya or something. She held the apple cupped in her palm, and stroked it gently with the forefinger of her other hand, so gently, as one would stroke a baby bird. Her knuckles were swollen; she was five months older than he was, and the arthritis had caught hold of her hard. He yearned to kiss those lumpy knuckles, gently, just the slightest brush of his lips. He ached for her to touch his face the way she touched the apple's dried-out skin.

"What do I have to do?" he whispered.

She didn't answer, didn't glance at him. She could love a shrunken old apple, she could love a caterpillar slowly inching through the grass, she could love a bee in flight or stray dog that stared with hungry eyes from across four lanes of traffic; she could love every living thing in the world, it seemed, except him.

"I didn't do anything wrong." He raised his hands to his chin, felt the roughness, days of unshaved whiskers scraping the pads of his fingers, and let his arms fall again. *Can I change?* he wondered. Is that what it'll take, is that what she wants? We used to talk. We used to laugh together. His hands, fists now, quivered at his sides. "I'll be an apple for you!" he shouted, and she looked up then. Their eyes met. Her flat, gray gaze held a challenge.

And in the challenge, he saw a glimmer of surprise, and maybe of hope.

He walked out into the garden. It was fall; the land was brown and bleak, dormant, a hibernation that looked like death, but it was in the garden that he would be able to do it, if it could be done anywhere. If it could be done at all. He let his hands relax, he let his arms relax. He took a deep breath. He knelt and touched the earth. His eyes open, his heart pounding, he bent his head and tried to make his life come true.

Turning, or Turning

†

It wasn't that Alberico wanted to turn liquid. Exactly. So much. It was that a cold and sinking feeling gripped him at the thought of being left out. Omitted and excluded from everything that was coming. Had already arrived, for most. "Not just in my stomach. All over."

"A sinking feeling," Flore said.

"Yes."

"And you're cold."

"Yes." He'd called her to tell her how he felt. She had not once called him to tell him how she felt. But at least she answered the phone.

"All over."

"Right."

"You're sick," she said.

"It's not that kind of cold and sinking feeling." Flore was one of the most literal-minded women Alberico had ever known. But she had always been that way. He resolved not to let go of his patience. That she was also the only person in the world willing to talk to him about this, albeit on the phone, was a factor that carried a lot of weight and gained more and more of it as the days and weeks accumulated. So, no yelling. No sarcasm.

"I know what kind it is," she said, and that threw him, for he had been bracing himself to hear her say that he should take some aspirin. Flore lived across town. Sometimes, talking to her, Alberico felt he was dropping his voice down a string connecting two paper cups, the phone only a simulacrum of a communication device. Since the turning had begun, or since they'd realized it had begun, Flore had refused to leave her apartment. She wasn't the only one. Sheltering in place had become fashionable among the nonchanging. She said, "You should be afraid of this, not longing for it. Normal people don't long for things like this."

"I don't know," he said. "I'm not sure what's happening is bad. I'm not saying it's good. But it's happening, and I think when everything shakes out…"

"You're going to be on the outside looking in."

"Yes."

"No date to the prom."

"Flore—"

"The wet people will have parties and they won't invite you."

"The wet people are going to be everybody," he said. "Looks like it, Flore. Except for a couple here, a couple there. We'll be—" Nothing, he thought. We'll be absolutely nothing. He didn't say that to Flore.

"It's a disease. It's a disease and they'll discover a treatment, a cure. We'll be what? Lucky to have escaped infection. Lucky to have stayed normal."

"I don't think it's a disease."

He'd talked to them, the wet people, the people turning liquid. He hadn't barricaded himself in his apartment. As the days and weeks accumulated, Alberico continued going to work, continued going to the store, continued running in the park, continued inviting friends for drinks, though his supervisor barely acknowledged his presence, the shops were empty of the dry, the park was full of the mad, and most of his friends were turning wet and, while polite enough, always, always had other plans.

"I think it's just something that happened. That has happened," he said. "It's not going to go away."

"I read online that scientists are trying to isolate a virus."

"There's no virus."

There was no virus. The change had gone worldwide in days, if not hours. Or had started worldwide, everywhere at the same time, but had taken longer to be noticed in some places, or longer to be reported.

"Sweating can be a symptom of infection. Or poisoning. A toxic spill. Or, god knows, something escaped from a lab somewhere."

No.

"They're not sweating," he said. "You know that."

Flore was silent for a long time.

"Do you remember the first one you saw?"

"No," she said, which startled him again, for he hadn't expected her to lie. He tried to find some mitigation for her dissembling. Perhaps she meant that on the first occasion in which the wet people had come to her attention, she'd seen many of them, so that technically there was no first *one*. Certainly it had taken some folks a while to catch on—the unobservant, the non-computer users, non-TV watchers. Flore owned three computers and two television sets, but Alberico could testify under oath how unobservant she was. Once when they were walking together, she'd missed a fifty-dollar bill, neatly folded in half, on the pavement. She'd stepped on it, and hadn't seen what it was. He teased her about that day. Used to tease her about it.

"I remember the first one I saw."

"Yeah. Belt-loop. You told me."

The first one Alberico had seen had been a hefty man walking a few steps ahead of him on the street he took from the bus station to work. A tall guy. Not too young, with thinning hair. Not too fit, with a big sloppy belly. The only thing that made Alberico glance at the man twice was the white washcloth, the same kind of washcloth his mother would hang on the rack next to the bathroom sink. The man's washcloth was threaded through one of the front belt-loops of his pleated khaki pants. He'd never seen that before, a washcloth pulled through a belt-loop. At the time, he'd thought it was possible that he was spotting a new trend, except that a washcloth through a belt-loop was such a stupid item to sport. Not that that had ever stopped a trend before. However, in the course of human history, while the aging and unfit might follow a trend, they very rarely began one. He'd decided he'd seen something idiosyncratic: unusual enough to mark, but not to dwell on.

The second one had been sitting next to him, in the window seat, on the bus on his way home. A woman, older than the man on the street, with short black hair, reading some sort of religious publication. In her lap, a white washcloth, the same type the man had had, which she picked up and then put down again before flipping each newsprint page of her tract. She hadn't looked at him. He hadn't spoken to her. But he had spent the entirety of the ride in contemplation.

"Let me come over," he said to Flore. "Please."

"No. You probably have it."

He didn't, whatever *it* was. Half the world, or it could be three-quarters, or it could be closer to eighty percent, did.

He had been repelled, at first. Well, not at first, because at first it was just the washcloths, at first it was only hands, and the liquid that seeped from them, at first, seeped slowly. A washcloth sopped it up easily. Folks wiped their hands, and wiped their hands, and went on with their business. At first it had just seemed a little peculiar, so many people with sweaty hands, in the spring.

It wasn't sweat. It wasn't lymph or blood turned suddenly colorless or any sort of previously recognized bodily fluid. It was mostly water, but not entirely water. It was slick—one might fairly say oily—and as the days and weeks accumulated (like bricks walling off the old world from the new) the wetness spread up from the hands and sleeved the arms, flowed down to cape backs and drape chests, sheathed legs, swathed feet. All around him, people were turning wet, turning liquid, and indeed, Alberico had been repelled. It did not look attractive. He did not imagine it felt very pleasant, either, to be wet all the time, like an amphibian. The washcloths were abandoned as the wetness expanded, and for a bit people walked around in dripping clothes. And then the clothes were abandoned, and nudity became standard, even on cool days, even on chilly days. The naked people didn't seem to feel cold. Alberico never saw any of them shiver.

Those who were not turning wet, turning liquid, became even more easily identifiable.

Alberico stopped feeling that twitch of disgust at the sight or thought of slicked flesh, of the sight or thought of unnatural liquid seeping from altered pores. The changing people did not manifest any distress; the mad who gathered in the park were men and women like himself: dry, unchanged, unable to live with the new way of things.

Every morning when he woke, he examined his hands.

"Please," he said to Flore. "It isn't something you can catch."

He had taken to waking four or five times a night, and each time, eyes closed, he drew fingers over fingers, slid palm across palm, checking for the beginning of the change. It began with the hands. With everyone who changed, it began with the hands. It did not begin for him.

Eighty percent. Perhaps more. News reports were unreliable, when they were not outright lies. Scientists searching for a virus. It was possible that among the twenty percent or so not affected, there were a few scientists wasting time in laboratories. More likely such accounts were simply attempts by a few of the twenty percent to keep the rest of the twenty percent calm.

In the park where Alberico ran, the mad sobbed and shouted, and battered each other.

The wet people did not sob, or shout, or attack one another, or not any more than people always had.

"Does it hurt?" he found himself asking, addressing a complete stranger, a stocky man with a mild expression who was checking his email on a street corner, the words rushing out of Alberico's mouth before he had time to become too nervous. The fluid covering the man's body was several centimeters thick; the pavement around his feet caught the slow drips. The man did not react.

"Sir? Excuse me?"

Finally the man looked up from his smart phone, his mild face puzzled. "Are you talking to me?"

"Does it hurt?"

"Does what hurt?"

"Is it uncomfortable?"

"I'm sorry," the man said, shoulders rising in a small shrug, and at the same moment moving away.

As a last shot, Alberico tried, "Are you cold?"

"It's a nice day," the man said, neutrally, his back to him.

It didn't freeze, this fluid. Alberico discovered that on television broadcasts. Not news reports, or not news reports about the change. The change wasn't news anymore to those who had changed. He realized it from crowd scenes, naked people nonchalant in the snow, then a close-up on the reporter, then a cut to the crowd, then back to our correspondent, the fluid sheathing all of them, thick and glistening. All right, the liquid froze a little bit, where it coated hair; he saw a reporter toss her head as she was wrapping up, *Back to you in the studio*, and lose some strands as they struck her shoulder and snapped off. But many, female and male, were depilating their heads now, so that wouldn't be a problem for a lot of people.

Alberico approached other strangers, shyer about bothering people he'd once known than interacting with people he'd never seen before and likely would never see again, though shy about that as well. He grew bolder as he suffered no consequences other than a few bits of rudeness, and grew more despondent as he came to understand how indifferent the wet people were to him. The wet people seemed equally indifferent to the change that had flowed out from their own bodies to alter everything.

They weren't bothered. It seemed to Alberico that most of them hardly noticed, as before most people hardly noticed their typically dryish skins. Unless some bruise or abrasion or itch called attention to itself, they hardly noticed their clothes, unless some article was too tight, or too loose, or too long, or too short. They weren't bothered because to them the changes had become normal. No one felt the need to wipe the fluid away any longer. What was, was, and what had been was vague in the memory, the way that it was hard to recollect exactly what a zero-degree day felt like in the midst of an August heat-wave.

He saw thickly slick couples walking and chatting, holding hands, kissing. Bus doors whooshed open, and fluid flowed out. The streets were soaked, the earth was soaked. He wondered about the children that would be born of wet parents. He wondered what was happening to those couples in which one had turned wet and the other hadn't. Or to the single child who remained dry in a family in which everyone else had changed.

"I'm lonely," Alberico whispered into the phone.

"So dump a couple of buckets of water over yourself and go play with your new friends."

"Flore," he said, in despair. He'd told her how he'd spoken to the wet people; he'd told her about examining his hands. She was the only person left who would talk to him. He hadn't told her about kneeling on the sidewalk and touching his fingertips to the freshest drops, about sitting in sopping bus seats, about taking off his clothes on a day that had been sunny and not terribly chilly and brushing against ten, twenty, forty strangers.

That he had given in to such impulses made Alberico fear that soon he would snap into lucidity for an instant and find himself in the park, sobbing with the rest of the mad.

"I'm coming over," he said.

Flore said, "I won't let you in."

She didn't. He'd known she wouldn't. Cross-town buses ran only once an hour after ten p.m., so he walked, knowing that she would not allow him into her apartment, knowing she wouldn't even open her window and talk to him as he stood on the sidewalk, but he walked quickly the whole way there, and he rang her bell several times, and he stood below her window and waved just in case she was lurking behind the blinds. It was better than going to the park.

When he got home he went straight to bed. The extra exercise didn't keep his sleep from breaking four times during the night; he rubbed his hands, and could not find any reason to hope that the change was beginning. He had known he wouldn't. In the morning, he scrutinized them, backs and fronts and between the fingers, but they were the same as they'd always been. He had known they would be.

When he got up to make his way to the bathroom, his left foot, the first one he set on the floor, shot out from under him and Alberico landed back on his bed, startled, shaken, and in pain from where his hip had struck the edge of the bed frame. Sitting up, he took a deep breath. He rubbed his hip. He'd never gotten around to getting a nice rug for the bedroom, so he had no rug at all. Better nothing than something tawdry. He put his right foot on the hardwood and slid it back and forth.

Oh dear.

He lowered himself to his hands and knees and examined the floor. The floor hadn't changed from last night. There was nothing wrong with the floor. There was nothing different about the floor. When he ran his hand over it, he encountered the expected amount of friction. Also the expected amount of detritus, as he hadn't vacuumed in a while.

Only after checking the floor did Alberico allow himself to think about the other possibility.

When he tried to get up, his feet slipped frictionlessly over the floor. He had to get back on his knees, swivel around, and hoist himself on the bed with his arms. He pushed himself back, and drew his feet up, one at a time, into his lap.

They weren't wet. They hadn't begun to exude liquid.

They were dry, and the slipperiest things he had ever felt. Grasping them was impossible. Sole and instep possessed the same lack of friction. He had to hold his ankle to turn the foot this way or that, though there was nothing, really, to see.

Slippery. I am turning slippery. And then there was a moment of utter dread when he wondered how that would be, how he could ever manage when the rest of his body changed. He'd slide off chairs, he wouldn't be able to pick anything up, or open doors; he'd be helpless. Then he told himself that this was only the first day, the first hour of the first day, the first minutes of that first hour. The people turning liquid had gone through the same terror before living inside coats of oily fluid had become normal. The washcloths. The washcloths had been abandoned.

On the night table, his phone vibrated.

In a few days, in a few weeks—in a few months at the most—his new state would feel completely normal to him. Would be completely normal to him. It could be fun, even. Right. Probably, with a little practice, he could glide around like a skater. And meanwhile, he'd put on some shoes. Gloves, too, when that became necessary. They would be his washcloths. All right. But he didn't imagine that this change would turn out to be the sort that shielded someone from the cold. He'd still be a clothed person in a mostly naked world. He'd be slippery, when everybody else wasn't. He was turning, but he wasn't turning wet.

The phone vibrated.

He picked it up. He could still do that. That was still all right.

It was Flore, of course. She was the only person who still talked to him.

"Alberico," she said. She was trying not to cry, and failing. "Flore, what is it?"

"I can't walk," she sobbed. "I keep falling down."

Alberico lowered the phone, then raised it again. "It's all right," he said. Flore let out a choked wail. "It's going to be all right," he said. "The washcloths were abandoned." The cold and sinking feeling returned for an instant, but he pushed it away. They would be a small group, in terms of percentage, even if all the non-wet people were turning slippery. It might be a small one in numbers, too, if only a fraction were. At this moment, he thought, others might be growing diamonds on their ribs or discovering they could fly. "Flore, it's not the end of the world." Well, it was, but it was also the beginning of a new one. He listened to Flore fighting back her panic, and loved her fiercely for that courage. "We're going to be all right," Alberico said, as, slowly, Flore's breathing grew calmer. He felt a warmth spreading through him, a sudden burgeoning sensation of relief, and hope, for a part in the future and for a tribe of his own.

THE OGRE'S WIFE

SHE DOES TRY TO SAVE THEM, BOTH THE BOYS AND THE girls, all the lost, sad, wandering children, those who are running from something, or toward something they cannot even vaguely describe. Many are so afraid that dragging a single word from their mouths is sweatier work than carding straw; the majority are so desperate that her only possible offer, that of hiding them in the tiny room behind the pantry, inside the chest, beneath the winter blankets, sounds good. Sounds like salvation. They barely flinch when, if, they recognize the meat turning on the spit, for the pantry is behind the kitchen, and to get to the small storeroom, the kitchen must be traversed. Most of them have traversed worse, or think they have.

She even tries to save the thieves, the sly boys and girls who come sidling along with their fresh rags and new-minted tales of woe, drawn by the stories of gold, of treasure, of hoarded jewels and coins and magic this and enchanted that. She knows these children wish only to steal, she can tell as soon as she sees their eyes, but it makes no matter. She hides them, she helps them, she feeds them what she eats herself, and she loads them with all the advice they will bear. Most of it they shrug off. She knows this, too, that no one will heed, that they will be guided by nothing but their own greed (the thieves) or their fear (the silent ones) or their desperation (the ones who have run the soles of their feet bloody). So it was with her; she was one of them, once.

Not like the one hiding in the chest now, obediently quiet, compliantly still, his scent disguised by the fresh rushes she has strewn on the floors of every room and the soap she is boiling in the foreyard. The wind is blowing the right way; the distracting smells she has created will certainly be enough to fool her children, and quite possibly enough to fool her husband as well.

The boy now curled in the chest is nearly a man grown, and has been fed well through most of his growth, even if not recently; his bones are strong, though his flesh is scant, and his teeth are as white as new snow. He has come to steal, believing the gaudy stories told around inn fires, told during the long summer nights up in the high pastures, told in the shade when the reapers rest from their labors. Gold, gems, a magic drum that beats out a prince's fortune at every blow, a cape of shadows that renders the wearer as imperceptible as a shadow himself, charmed boots that can carry a person across every mountain and every sea, a white flower whose petals turn to diamonds at each sunrise. Treasure upon treasure piled up in the ogre's house. He has heard all these tales, and he believes them. He wants these riches; he aches for them. He is risking his life, and she, the ogre's wife, wishes him well. Desperation drives him, as it drives the others, the lost, the silent, the runaways. Each of them has a tale, and each is different, and all of them are the same.

Her own father was desperate, when he sold her to the ogre. Not this one, not this husband, but her first, the one with the strength of twenty men and the appetite of a hundred, with a beard down to his knees and shoulders as broad across as a herring boat's keel, with a sword as heavy as a hundred-year oak belted at his waist and one golden hair on his bald head, with a nose like a flattened hand and teeth like gnarled black roots, with silver clinking in his purse and a penis that tore her so badly she bled for weeks and weeks. Though that came later. Her mother, she remembers, cursed her father, cursed him in her soft, powerless voice, and threw her apron over her head. Her curses came louder then, with her face hidden. Her father simply nodded, his eyes down, not looking at the ogre, nor at his wife, nor at the daughter he was selling, nor at his other children, gathered in wonder and fear, silent, shaking, watching, their terror more for themselves than for their sister, for that is the way of human beings, and there was nothing they could have done for her, anyway. She screamed when her father held out his palm and let the ogre drop the coins into it; when her father closed his hand and nodded again, she cursed him as her mother was cursing him, and worse; just before the ogre touched her for the first time, she spat into her father's face. But the ogre picked her up and carried her off, and that was that.

She was twelve, or perhaps thirteen, then. It's strange, she thinks, as she sits and listens to the soap boil (for the soap-pot is enchanted and needs no stirring or tending; she can sit in the front room and embroider headdresses for her daughters, or knit stockings for her sons, or simply sit and watch the clouds float across the sky, and the soap will make itself) what one can remember and what one cannot. She can remember her mother's voice, but not her face; she can remember her father's face, but not the touch of his hand; she can remember her first husband's penis and his one golden hair, but not the color of his eyes. Her little brothers and sisters she remembers hardly at all. She hopes they have not been among the desperate ones who have come to the ogre's house; or, if they have, that they have been among the few who have escaped detection. She doesn't remember how many brothers and sisters she had before her father sold her; she assumes her mother bore several more after the last time she saw her.

It was ten years before the boy came, the boy who wanted to rescue her, the boy who wanted to be a hero. That she remembers; ten years with her first husband.

She was wise already, after ten years. The boy was beautiful, with sparkling black eyes and skin as soft as flour, but that made no matter. You're not strong enough, she said. He'll snap you like a quill. Go home, marry a girl from your village, be happy.

Tell me the ogre's secret, the boy said. You must know it. How can he be defeated, how can he be destroyed?

Of course I know it, she said. The ogre can be killed only by his own sword, the sword of bronze as heavy as a barn, that hangs on the wall above my spinning wheel when it is not hanging from his belt. You will never be able to lift it, not you even with the help of twenty like you; you will never be able to swing it, not you even with the help of thirty like you. You must cut off the ogre's head with one stroke, and as it is still rolling and bleeding, you must shear the single golden hair from his head. This you cannot do, not you, not even with the help of forty like you. Go home. Live. The gold is not worth your life.

It is not gold I come for, the beautiful boy said, but you. I love you.

You love me? This seemed so unlikely she almost burst into laughter, which would have been an unkindness, for the boy was solemn, nearly trembling in his earnestness.

I love you, he said, and I shall slay the ogre and rescue you.

He went away then, and she watched him go, slim hips, swinging arms, rough-cut brown hair, until he disappeared around a turn in the road, and she did not see him again for a year.

When he returned, he came boldly, beating at the front door with a hard fist, for he had been to a wise woman, or a woman who said she was wise, and had taken twelve drinks of a potent potion, one each month, to make him strong enough to lift the ogre's sword. When she opened the door, he rushed in past her, to snatch the sword off the wall. But he was not strong enough yet; the wise woman's potion had not done its full work, and after a moment, arms quivering, he dropped the sword. The ogre looked up from his dinner, grease ringing his mouth, and belched laughter. The boy, whom she scarcely recognized, ran.

It is strange what one remembers and what one cannot remember. The second time the boy came, the first time he had tried to fight the ogre, he was taller than the first time she'd seen him, when he spoke to her as she stood on one side of the threshold and he stood on the other, when she had watched him striding away with pity and longing in her heart. His shoulders were broader, too, and his thighs. His hips were no longer slim. She could not be sure, now, if his nose had flattened like an open hand, or if his teeth had begun to twist like old roots, that first time he had returned.

Who was that, her first husband asked, slow and sated after his meal, and she had answered, I don't know, and it had almost been the truth.

The boy came back after another twelve months, and that time he had held the sword well, and swung it once, but the ogre, grinning, had blocked the blow with a careless, almost languid, motion of one arm. Then he plucked the sword from the boy's hand, tossed it into the air, caught it—by which time the boy had fled again. This time the ogre chased him for a mile or two, before losing interest. Fortunate for the boy that this time, too, he had come after the ogre had already stuffed his belly full ten times over.

But not boy, not any longer... she could not call him that, could not think of him that way any more. I love you, he cried, just before he ran, and that earned her a beating from her husband when he came home, out of breath and with an ache in his bowels and sweat pouring from his bald head, but the boy was not the beautiful youth who had spoken to her across the threshold. He looked like the ogre's younger brother.

She was very wise then, twelve years an ogre's wife, and if her first husband did not know what the future held, she did. She lay awake at night and tears pooled in her eyes, but she did not let them fall, for then the ogre would question her, and the less they spoke, the easier it was for her not to take a knife, one of the many sharp kitchen knives, and open her veins.

The next time the boy who was no longer a boy returned, she saw at once that he must have downed a vat of the potion concocted by the wise woman, or the woman who said she was wise. He was as tall as the ogre, as broad as the ogre, as strong as the ogre, as hungry as the ogre, as ugly as the ogre, as terrible as the ogre. He took the sword off the ogre's belt, tore it free through the scabbard with no more effort than a child would spend tearing a leaf, and cut off the ogre's head with a single blow, and sheared off the one golden hair before the head had bounced across the floor three times. Then he turned to her and grinned, and it was the same grin she had seen when her first husband had dropped three or four coins into her father's open hand.

I love you, he said, and she swallowed her own spit and bowed her head.

She and her first husband had not had any children. With the second, they came one after the next. At the birth of each, boy or girl, the ogre was gleeful, and celebrated with barrels of ale and the flesh of twenty men, roasted, boiled, fried... it made no matter.

The children took after their father. The ogre who had once been a beautiful brave boy roared with pride. She kept silent, and polished the kitchen knives. The children grew quickly, and were the terror of the countryside, and each year or two a new one fought his or her way out into the light from between her legs. She smothered one or two, starved a couple, but still they came, one after another, like their father, all like their father, and she could not stop her eyes filling with tears, but she never let one drop fall.

And still the other children come, the desperate ones, the ones running from something more terrible than any ogre's house, the ones hiding from someone more terrible than any ogre, the ones seeking for riches that would free them from a life more terrible than they imagined the life of an ogre's wife could be.

She cannot remember how many children she has. She knows they will all be home soon, hungry, roaring, wanting food, eager for dinner. Dinner is cooking. She can smell it, despite the rushes and the boiling soap. She cannot smell the young thief hidden in the chest beneath the winter blankets. She hopes he will remain unfound, that he has heard at least a few words of the advice she has given him, that he will snatch one object, the blue-feathered fowl which craps rubies, perhaps, and escape with it, and be satisfied. She does not want to be turning the kitchen spit tomorrow, with the young thief's body on it, roasting slowly over the fire.

But she will turn the kitchen spit tomorrow, with the young thief's body on it, or another's body, hunted and brought back alive by her children or her second husband. There will be many bodies to roast tomorrow. Or boil, or fry, or stew. It made no matter. One way or the other, the family must be fed.

She would save them all if she could.

She does what she can, and she knows herself as terrible as her husband, as both her husbands, though she has never once tasted human flesh, as terrible as her children, though she has not chosen this, did not chose this, would never have chosen this.

She has bowed her head and kept silent.

She bows her head and keeps silent.

In the chest, the boy, the thief, is silent. He believes the stories of riches, of wealth unimaginable, of magic, and why should he not? They are all true.

She has saved a few. Twelve years with her first husband, more than twenty with her second, she has saved a few of the young and lost, the young and adventurous, the young and dreadfully hurt. She sits in the front room, dinner almost ready, the soap almost solid, the rushes fresh and fragrant, and hates herself ten times more than she hates her father.

The children will come home first, and then her husband.

The boy, the thief, lies in the chest, as still as a live boy can lie.

She sits, the ogre's wife, listening for footsteps.

How not to Apologize to a Scarecrow

Guiltily.

It's not your fault you bumped into it and knocked its stupid pigeon-beshat hat off. Yes, you saw it on your way to Tracy-Ann's place. For some dumbass reason there's a farmer's market in Lawrence Square every weekend from April until October. You saw the thing, old clothes plumped out with crumpled newspapers and some actual by-god straw, standing guard over the empty square as you passed. Someone had gone to a lot of trouble to set it up, to arrange it so it really looked like it was standing on its own, instead of being wired to the traffic-light pole. Urban art. The kind of shit people with generous grandmas and way too much time on their hands get up to. Gloves had been sewn to the ends of the scarecrow's flannel sleeves; the paper-stuffed jeans had been crammed into battered construction boots, the boots laboriously stapled to the denim. A lot of work, a ton of work. They'd done a good job, the artsy kids, even though the only bird this thing was likely to frighten was a severely retarded sparrow. Had to have been artists, maybe even the group from the cooperative gallery on Miranda Place, the one that wouldn't let Tracy-Ann show her shadowboxes, told her they were too derivative. The scarecrow's head was a smooth, painted pumpkin, sporting an expression of knowing amusement. It must have been attached to the torso somehow, because the head didn't topple when you banged into the art installation, just the hat. The hat went flying, landing upside down a few feet away, close to a pile of fresh dog shit. "Ah crap, I'm sorry," you say. "I didn't mean it. I wasn't looking where I was going. Sorry, man." You're swaying a little, and you pat the scarecrow's shoulder. It feels solid. "Sorry, shit, forgive me, please." You sound like a teenager who's broken Mom's new favorite garage-sale-find commemorative plate, the one she phoned all her sisters and cousins about, gloating over snagging it for next to nothing. The look on Mom's face when you knocked it off the table and it shattered into twelve pieces still haunts you. It was an accident, it wasn't your fault, but the guilt still belongs to you and you alone.

In her apartment, right now, Tracy-Ann is lying on the floor, on the knock-off Persian rug you'd bought her as a housewarming present five years ago. She is lying on her side, because you made sure to shift her into that position before you left. You figured it was safer to leave her on the floor than to try to hoist her on the bed. Once you'd seen her with a spectacular rainbow bruise on her forehead, which she claimed she'd received during a nightmare in which she dreamed she was falling, and somehow wound up diving off her futon and face-smacking the floor. You don't really believe this story. But the semester before you dropped out of college, one of the jocks on your dorm floor had passed out on his back after a party, puked in his sleep, choked on it, and died. In Tracy-Ann's apartment, which was two rooms in the basement of an illegally converted house, the empty cans of Bud were way outnumbered by the empty bottles of Stoli. You turned her on her side. Tracy-Ann is your sister. You are four years older. You are the one who gave her her first drink. That is not the worst thing you ever did to her.

The scarecrow bends its painted pumpkin head. Its magic-marker eyes are oval, friendly. Its eyebrows are arched, quizzical. Its lips are closed, but curved. It was painted to smile. You begin to turn, to go pick up the hat, but the scarecrow's gloved right hand is closed around your left wrist. The scarecrow is wearing leather gloves.

Angrily.

THIS IS NOT YOUR FUCKING FAULT. WHO THE FUCK PUTS A scarecrow up in the middle of a city square, anyway? And okay, maybe you weren't looking real close at where you were going, but how come there was only one fucking light in Lawrence Square that worked, anyway? Two o'clock in the morning, there's supposed to be some illumination. You paid taxes for shit like that, right? But the only functioning light was all the way on the north side of the square. Even the traffic light the stupid scarecrow was wired to didn't work. This is how accidents happen. This is how kids get killed, goddammit. "Fuck," you say, too loud for two in the morning, but who the hell cared, "sorry about the fucking hat, okay, but if there were any freaking lights on around here I would've fucking seen you. You don't fucking belong here, anyway, you know that? Fucking scarecrow. Give me a break. Okay, okay, I'll get your fucking hat. Just fucking let go."

In Tracy-Ann's apartment, you tried to talk to her. You'd gone there, with a bag of groceries from the convenience store, pissed because a can of fucking spaghetti-o's cost a buck fifty in that rip-off joint, and never mind how much they gouged you for bread, but buying the stuff anyway because the last time you'd seen Tracy-Ann, just by chance, on the street in front of the thrift shop, she looked like she couldn't have weighed more than ninety pounds, down jacket and platform sneakers included. Your mutual father had tormented her for years with his *crisco in a can* and *thunderthighs*, and you hadn't helped at all. You'd laughed, too. When Tracy-Ann cried, you'd laughed harder, all the time with one eye on Dad, making his grin your own. A couple of hours ago, when Tracy-Ann finally opened the door and let you in, she took the bag of groceries and dropped it on the floor. You screamed at her. "Eat, goddammit! Do you want to die? What the fuck is wrong with you? I got a moron for a sister. There are faster ways to commit suicide, you cunt. Eat something!" Tracy-Ann cracked open a fresh bottle of Stoli. You screamed some more, then took a couple of slugs yourself. But you stayed. You stayed, until she passed out. And you left so furious you could barely see straight.

The scarecrow's grip on your wrist is as strong as a vise. One time, when you were only eight, Dad put your hand in a vise. Dad had had a workshop out in the garage. He used to pretend to make stuff. Dollhouses, birdhouses. None of his projects had ever emerged from the garage. You were twelve before you figured out that he was lying about making things out there. The day he broke your hand, you'd done something. Brought home a B on a spelling test, answered back, forgotten to kiss him goodnight. Something. He dragged you out into the garage and mashed your hand in the vise. He did it grimly, without even a shadow of a smile on his face. You refused to scream, but you cried. You couldn't help it. You were only eight. Mom didn't come out to rescue you. You were eight, so you still believed that was possible, that she might do that. Tracy-Ann hid in her room. She was four. What the hell else was she going to do? Finally, finally you did scream. You screamed at Dad, "I'm sorry, okay? I'm fucking sorry! Fuck you! I'm sorry!" And for that, for saying the f-word, he broke your other hand. The scarecrow is holding on just like that, that tight, that hard. If you try to pull away, you know that bones must break.

Insincerely.

"I'm so very, very sorry," you say. "Let me make it up to you." You stop tugging, stop trying to wrest your wrist free. You look directly into the scarecrow's narrow painted eyes. "You're wonderful, a true original, an authentic piece of art, and I'm scum, you know? I'll do anything you want.

I'll get your hat back. I'll buy you a new hat. I love you. I'm not just saying that. I love you. You're very important to me. Just give me a chance to prove it. You'll see. You won't be sorry. Things will be different from now on. I'll never hurt you again. I'll never hurt your feelings, ever. Really. Please? You can believe me. I promise." You swallow. Your mouth is very dry. This spitlessness makes your throat click. "I'll be your friend. From now on. I promise. I'll be your friend."

In her apartment, after they sat down on her saggy futon, after they cracked open the Stoli, after Tracy-Ann staggered around for a while and discovered that there truly was no ice, after you'd offered to go back to the convenience store for a bag, after she told you to fuck yourself, *yeah, once you're out the door you're not coming back, you think I don't know you? I know you, you fucker*, after she dropped her scarcely ninety pounds down on the opposite side of the futon, Tracy-Ann said, "Never once. I couldn't count on you, ever. We lived in that same house for fifteen years. And you never helped me, ever. So I don't know what you're doing here now." *I'm sorry*, you said. *But come on, it wasn't as bad as all that, was it?* Tracy-Ann took a long drink, and passed you the bottle. *I was a kid, too*, you said. "You were older," she said. "I hoped you'd protect me. I hoped for so damn long. But you never did, not once. You protected yourself." *Dad hit me*, you protested. *He broke my fucking hands. He—* "I would rather have been hit," she said, and you dropped the subject. You and she drank some more. Something very melancholy began to burgeon in your heart, a pressure that rose and made the back of your eyeballs ache. You had to say something or else start crying, and if you cried in front of Tracy-Ann, you would hate yourself forever. "I'm sorry," you said. "Can we start again? Can we be friends?" "No," she said. "I love you," you said, though it wasn't true. "I don't love you," she said, and you knew that was true.

The scarecrow reaches out and takes hold of your other wrist. The scarecrow doesn't believe you any more than Tracy-Ann did. Its legs, plump in its ragged jeans, come loose from the traffic-light pole.

Desperately.

THE SCARECROW WRAPS ITS ARMS AROUND YOU. IT HUGS tight. Its pumpkin head is not smiling. It has opened its painted lips. Its painted teeth grin. Its eyes are cold and knowing. "Please, no," you beg. "I'm sorry, I'm sorry. Please, I'll do anything. I mean it, I mean it! I was wrong! Please don't, please don't!" The scarecrow leans its pumpkin head down, places its painted mouth next to your ear, and bites it off.

"Fuck you!" you yelled at Tracy-Ann. "Dad and Mom did worse than me. What the fuck do you want? I'm making a fucking effort here. This is the last time, you hear me? You can rot. You can choke on your own puke and die. I'm not trying any more. I'm sorry! Stop fucking blaming me!" Tracy aimed a level gaze at you, and said, evenly and remarkably soberly, considering how much she'd put away by then, "Dad and Mom are dead. You aren't. And you were older, and you were supposed to protect me. That's what I don't forgive you for. And you know what else?" She stood up, bottle in hand, holding it like she was preparing to swing it at your head. "You enjoyed it. As long as it wasn't you, you enjoyed it." You screamed then, really screamed, because that hurt, that hurt so much you knew it was true. You screamed *I'M REALLY FUCKING SORRY*, and Tracy-Ann threw the almost-empty bottle at you, and missed, and then she not-so-slowly lowered herself to the floor, flopped on her back, and passed out. You turned her over on her side.

The scarecrow is off the pole. Its arms and legs are gripping you like a straightjacket. The side of your head is gushing blood; you know the ear is gone. Hot wetness is soaking your neck, your jacket. The pain is starting to hit, not all of it yet, just the tip of it, the very beginning. You are still in shock; shock cushions pain. Even so, you start to cry. The scarecrow slides its smooth pumpkin head across your face, and bites off your chin. You can still talk, though, and you ask, desperately, "My fault? Really? My fault?" The scarecrow does not answer. It seems that, though it can bite, and grip, and hurt, it cannot speak. The scarecrow slides its head up. It whacks its pumpkin forehead into your skin-and-bone forehead. In your mind, you hear *we are each of us responsible for the harm we might have prevented*. It sounds like something from one of the textbooks you never read before you dropped out of college. You don't believe this. You think this is a crock of shit. You believe that you are responsible only for the harm you have actually personally done, you your own damn self. But the scarecrow is an adherent of a different philosophy, and the scarecrow has all four limbs constricted around you, pinning you to a spot on the pavement in Lawrence Square, and blood is soaking your clothes, and there is no one about, not one single live human being awake and walking the streets of the city, not at this hour, not in this neighborhood. There is no help anywhere. There will be no rescue.

Wordlessly.

I WAS ONLY TRYING TO SAVE MYSELF, YOU WANT TO SAY. *I was just trying to survive. Was that so awful, so unforgivable?* But you cannot give voice to these words, for the scarecrow darts its grinning head forward and rips out your throat.

In Tracy-Ann's apartment, after you turned her over on her side, you stood for a couple of minutes, just staring down at her. She'd fucked up her life. And yeah, you'd fucked up your life, too, but at least you hadn't fucked it up as badly as she had. We lived in the same house, you thought, we had the same parents, we went through the same shit. I learned to deal. You didn't. Well, too bad for you. I tried. Once we were both grownups, once we were both out of there, I tried. I bought you that fucking rug you're lying on. I brought you a bag of groceries today, and you tossed them in a corner. You're a loser, and I'm not. I'm sorry, Tracy-Ann, but that's it. I'm not coming back here. I have to take care of myself, and seeing you just brings me down. I need to think of myself first. That's the way the world works. I am not responsible for any of this. Sorry.

You didn't say any of this out loud. You just left, shutting the door quietly behind you.

The scarecrow chews through your throat. Your vision fades; everything is dark gray, dotted with the occasional yellow sparkle. You hate the yellow sparkles. Even if you wanted to say something now, a protest, an excuse, a vow to change, to try again, even a sincere apology or a mindful admittance of fault, you cannot. It is too late. Your rage swells, then fades, replaced by grief. The grief is for yourself, mostly; only a little of it is for Tracy-Ann. You deserve more—more time, more chances, more motherfucking slack. You are not a bad person. How the fuck do you get to merit this? Then the grief fades, ebbing into sorrow, dying into numbness, and the grayness becomes deep black, no yellow sparkles even, and fuck you miss the little bastards now they're gone forever, and the black becomes emptiness, and there is nothing left before the last second but a brief, fleeting, exquisitely painful acceptance of failure.

Fugly

IT BROKE IN THROUGH THE BATHROOM WINDOW, THE ONE they never opened, the narrow window to the left of the sink that looked out on the blank wall of the building next door. When they'd first moved in, Lenore had tacked a dishtowel to the frame, in order to spare them the sight of the chewed-up bricks. Pete had bitched and bitched about that towel. Fucking ugly, he called it. He'd pissed and moaned until she finally found the right-sized curtain rod at an odd-lots store and hung a genuine curtain from it. Beige. Frilly. Dotted with yellow flowers. She knew he'd hate it. The day she put it up, Pete came home late. Again. She waited in silence until he went to take a leak; when he came out, she dared him with her eyes to say anything. He hadn't let out a peep about the curtain. Since then she'd ignored the window. Forgotten about it, really. So had Pete. Out of sight, out of mind. All the things they fought about, that wasn't one of them. A dead issue.

It broke in. He couldn't blame her for that.

The first *crack* woke her. The night was just hitting two, but Lenore came out of sleep alertly, no muzziness, no confusion. *Glass breaking. Glass being broken.* Pete an inert lump beside her. Then came the sound of glass falling on tile: *inside.* Someone breaking in, something coming inside. "Pete," she said, and hit his shoulder. She'd sat up automatically, was already sliding out of bed. "Pete, put on your shoes." Because there was broken glass.

She'd been in bed for an hour, reading a little, making a to-do list for the week, when he had finally come home, close-faced, taciturn. He'd half-nodded at her as he began to undress. No wisp of a scent that might have been perfume, no signs that he'd recently showered. His clothes were rumpled, but that wasn't unusual. "I asked you to stop by Green Stand, get some—" "I forgot, okay? Are you going to make a big deal about it *now*? I'll get it tomorrow." He wouldn't; Lenore jotted down another item on her list. She didn't speak to him again until the window broke.

Her own shoes on, standing next to the bed, she said again, "Pete. Get up. Put on your shoes." Not speaking softly, but not yelling. She wasn't afraid of robbers, of human attack; the bathroom window was too small, the space between their building and the one quietly crumbling next door too narrow, to accommodate a person.

"Wha…" he said, not stirring.

"Something broke the window in the bathroom." As she said it, more glass fell, a sharp tinkling on tile. Then came a thud. She swore. The thud sounded heavy enough for a possum, a raccoon… muskrat? One of those animals that didn't belong in cities, but which had turned urban scavengers out of necessity. Or maybe just the ordinary kind of rat, a big, red-eyed, rabid one.

"Dreaming," Pete said, which meant he thought she was, or was pretending to think so.

"Get up," she snapped, in her stop-being-a-child voice, and flipped on the light.

"What the fuck!" he roared.

Good. At least he was fully awake now.

Lenore left the bedroom. She switched on the hall light. The bathroom was only a few feet away, dark inside, of course; the door was half-open. Pete had been in there last. She bet the toilet seat was up, too.

She stood still, watching for movement, listening for the sound of claws on tile, or chittering, squeaks, whatever noises a scared animal might make. The light would have startled it; probably it had retreated to the darkest corner of the bathroom.

Did it have to be an animal? Lenore, keeping her breathing quiet, tried to think of what else it could be. A brick, coming loose from the wall of the building next door?

Probably not.

The best thing might be to just shut the bathroom door quickly, trap the creature. It couldn't get out if the door was closed. Go back to bed, deal with it in the morning. By morning, it might have found its way back out of the window. Unless, she thought, it was hurt. Then it would be lying on the tiles all night, suffering. And they'd still have to deal with it in the morning. And the broken glass.

They? Pete still hadn't gotten out of bed. He'd probably stuck his head under both pillows, hers as well as his, and was doing his damnedest to go back to sleep. It'd be no different in the morning. Now, or then, she'd have to handle it.

It wasn't a big deal that he'd forgotten to pick up the soy milk at Green Stand. Slipped his mind, that was all. The way the promise he'd made last week to meet her after work for dinner had slipped his mind. Over and done with, in the past. A dead issue.

Dead issue. Better than dead tissue. Lenore flinched. That had come of out of nowhere. She didn't want to think about that, not ever, but especially not now.

Pete, get your ass out of bed. They were supposed to be in this together, weren't they? This, this mess called life. Pete hadn't always been so... distant. They'd shared things, worked together. Side by side. Now, Lenore was always in the lead, dragging him along, his indifference a heavier weight than the hostility. She was a sled dog pulling an elephant. A sled dog whose sled had disintegrated, leaving only the traces intact.

Lenore edged toward the bathroom. So this was the plan: she'd hold the door with one hand, switch on the light with the other. Take a quick look. See if the creature was hurt, bleeding, anything like that. See what kind of animal it was. She did not fancy putting on gloves and grabbing a pillowcase to try to rescue a rat. Or a raccoon, for that matter. If the animal rushed her, tried to get out, she'd slam the door on it.

If she called the cops, would they come, she wondered, or would they just refer her to animal control? No one from animal control would show up before morning, that was for sure.

First things first. Lenore took hold of the doorknob. Poised on the balls of her feet, she reached in and hit the light switch.

Broken glass on the floor—she shot a look at the window: the pane had definitely been smashed from the outside. Nothing by the towel rack, nothing under the sink. Nothing, nothing… *shit.*

Something that size could never have fit through the window. Never.

Something that size could never had escaped her notice, even at the first, swift glance. It was right there in the middle of the bathroom, huddled against the toilet, eyes blinking. But she hadn't seen it. She hadn't seen it for at least three seconds.

Shut the door. The back part of her brain, insistent, but distant. Lenore didn't move.

Its respiration was ragged, each inhale a harsh rasp, each exhale accompanied by a low whimper. No way could she not have heard that in the corridor, or even just outside the bedroom. Clearly hurt, obviously in pain, it looked stunned, lost, terrified. There wa no blood, or at least none that Lenore could see, but then, right at that moment she wasn't trusting her perceptions all that much. "Holy mother of…" she said, and crouched down, her hand still on the doorknob. "What are you? Where did you come from?"

It was hairy, rather than furry, and lumpy. Misshapen. Lenore pushed away the word *deformed*. Limbs, yes, digits, yes, eyes and nose and a mouth, a torso; its genitalia were hidden, but Lenore had an impression of femaleness. For no real reason... perhaps its roundness? The limbs were round, the torso round. A balloon creature, but made of flesh. And old, she thought. Old. Its fur... its hair... was black, the silver-olive skin of its bare limbs unwrinkled, but age radiated from it, like heat.

Of course I'm dreaming, Lenore thought, very calmly. In the morning I'll tell Pete about this, and we'll laugh.

If Pete was there when she woke. He had so many early meetings these days. *I didn't kiss you goodbye because you were sleeping and I didn't want to disturb you.* So many late ones, too. *Sorry, I forgot to call. You're not going to make a big deal out of it, are you?* More and more, whenever she looked up, he wasn't there.

Maybe Pete was the dream, she thought, and shook her head sharply. Foolishness, middle-of-the-night chimeras. Stress. Old age creeping up on padded, clawed feet. Wake up, Lenore told herself. Her knees hurt from crouching; her hand ached from gripping the doorknob. There was something dying on her bathroom floor.

Once when she was in school a classmate had brought in a tiny baby bird, smaller than her thumb, a naked, quivering thing that had fallen from a nest and could never survive. Some of the kids had been disgusted, others had made 'oooh how cute' sounds. The child holding the dying baby bird had wept silently. Lenore couldn't remember the girl's name, but her eyes had held the same plea as the eyes of the creature on the bathroom floor: *help. I don't know what to do.* Lenore had taken the bird and killed it with a rock. She and the girl who found the baby bird had not been friends before; they were not friends afterward. Lenore killed the bird because no one else was going to.

"Is that what you want?" Lenore asked the dying creature. Naturally, she didn't expect it to answer. But wouldn't a quick ending be preferable to a long night of suffering?

Help. I don't know what to do.

Lenore let go of the doorknob, easing down from her crouch into a kneeling position. The tiles were cold and hard. "I'll help if I can," she said, "but I don't know what you want." Slowly, so as not to frighten it, she held out her arms. It wouldn't bite her, she believed. It didn't seem to have anything to bite with. Its soft-looking lips opened and closed on emptiness. Nor did it appear to have anything to scratch with. The digits on the ends of its limbs were round, smooth, nail-less. "Are you cold? Are you hungry?" There was no blood, still no blood that Lenore could see; that had to be a good thing. She tried not to dwell on broken bones, internal injuries. If it could move, walk to her, even crawl, then perhaps its pain and confusion were only from the shock of the fall. Maybe it hadn't come here to die; maybe all it needed was a little comfort. If it wouldn't move, then she would fetch a blanket, that green-striped one that Pete hated and so wouldn't bitch about. She could make a sort of nest for it, in the bathroom, with a cereal bowl for water, another bowl for milk, maybe (but there was no milk, Pete had forgotten to pick any up). No, it wouldn't come, it was too afraid; Lenore put her arms down, resting her fingertips gingerly on the cold tile (there was glass everywhere), and prepared to push herself up. It blinked at her, and she froze. Its mouth gaping and shutting like a stranded fish, it began to crawl, elbows and knees bent, soft fingers and toes spread, as if its own weight were nearly too much for it to shift, as if the gravity here were crushingly heavy. It avoided every sliver and fragment of broken glass; it crawled up to Lenore's knees, then climbed up onto her thighs, and she had to put her arms around it to keep it from slipping down again.

Warm. Almost hot, but not fever-hot; not a sickly, scary heat, but the warmth of a strong, healthy animal. Because of its roundness she'd imagined its body would be soft, even squishy, but it was firm, muscular under the roundness. Its black hair was bristly against the skin of her forearms. It pressed its head against her stomach, and wrapped its own limbs around her, and they came together perfectly, with a silent jigsaw-puzzle click, as if they were two parts of one whole, as if Lenore had created this being herself, a custom-made stranger, to fit her so neatly and exactly. She gasped in surprise, and breathed in only the scent of the bathroom, a whiff of bleach from the last time she'd cleaned it, a thread of apricot from the bottle of shampoo left uncapped in the shower caddy, a whisper of dankness from the smashed window and the dark narrow space between the buildings. In her arms, the stranger began to breathe more easily, and soon a low sound came from the center of its chest, something like a purr, something like a coo.

Lenore never knew how long they sat together. It seemed a very long time, and it was all too brief.

"What the fuck," Pete said, and he was in the bathroom, past Lenore, for she had shifted from kneeling to sitting, her back against the wall under the towel rack with the stranger on her lap, her arms around it. And now Pete was in the bathroom, horrified, disgusted, hands quickly clenched. He was wearing shoes.

"There's broken glass," Lenore said. "Could you get the brush and pan from the kitchen and sweep it up?" She thought it was quite a reasonable thing to ask, and besides, it would get him out of the bathroom for a moment. The other in her lap had stopped coo-purring. She didn't want it to be frightened. She didn't want Pete to be frightened, either.

"What the fuck are you doing? What the hell *is* that?"

"Pete, listen," Lenore said, very calmly, very reasonably, but he was already baring his teeth, and when the stranger in her lap moved—just lifted its head, all it did was lift its head—Pete kicked it. Kicked it while Lenore was holding it, kicked it as she tried to keep it snug and safe and warm. Lenore felt the shock of the impact through her whole body, from belly to spine to the ends of her toes. The other was catapulted out of her embrace, its bristly hair scratching her face as its own body flew up. It made no sound, but Lenore cried out.

Pete was shoving her back—she must have been rising, for him to push her down again—and the other was on the tiles, on the broken glass, and Pete stomped it, stomped it hard with his steel-toed boots, those boots he liked to wear to the office on dress-down Fridays. Lenore screamed.

The other shattered. Like glass, like ice, like china. Shattered into dozens of pieces, shards, slivers, fragments. The shards shimmered, reflecting the overhead light, running the rainbow spectrum in the flash of a second, and then all turned green. They all turned green.

Then they all leaped at Pete. As they flew up, the shards flickered, iridescent, like the feathers on a pigeon's neck. But when they sliced into him, they were green, slashing so fast, so keenly, Lenore was on her feet and reaching for him before the first red spurted.

"Pete!" *Why, why, why*: the word pounded in her head, but she didn't say it, just grabbed at the shards, snatched at them; they were slippery, and sharp, and they cut her, too, and her arms ran slick. But then the fragments and slivers and shards came together, and the other was in her arms again, heavy and warm and bristly, panting roughly, tense, but whole. For a second, just a second, Lenore thought everything would be all right.

Pete tore it out of her embrace and dashed it to the floor, and again it shattered, again the fragments shimmered and greened, and again they sprang up, at him. He tried to bat them away; he beat at them with his fists, knocking a few of them out of the air, and tried to crush the shards into powder under his heavy boots.

"Pete, no! Pete, no, no!"

The bathroom was awash in red and flickering with green, green, green.

Lenore swept all the slivers and fragments she could into her arms; at first it made no difference, the remaining pieces continued to attack him, but she kept on, determinedly, not letting go of any, despite the sharpness, the slickness, grabbing more, more, hugging them tight, until she reached a critical mass, the tipping point, and all the shards came together again, even the bits of crystalline powder from the soles of Pete's boots, all whole again in her embrace. It panted, heavily, and trembled so violently she was afraid it would shake apart again, all on its own. But as long as she held it, it held together.

"What are you doing?" Pete screamed. "What have you done?"

"I didn't do anything! It broke in!" *Why did you attack it, why did you try to kill it, it wasn't hurting you, it had almost fallen asleep on my lap, it wasn't doing anything, anything at all.* She bit everything back, stuffed the words down, because Pete was streaming blood, his face a red mask, his arms crimson sleeves, and so was she, she must have been, she could feel the wetness on her own skin, all over, and the thousand stings as pain broke through shock. "Alcohol," she muttered. "Bandages. There's ointment, too, in the cabinet." Pete wasn't listening, of course he wasn't, he never did, maybe that was why he thought she didn't pay attention to what he said, because he never paid any to her, but she had to help him, and to do that she had to put the visitor down. She whispered to it, "Just for a minute, just for a minute," because it was trembling, but Pete was bleeding, and she set it down.

And it shattered into a thousand green shards and launched every bit of itself at Pete.

"Bitch!" Pete screamed.

"I didn't! I just—" Lenore snatched at the slivers and splinters, grabbing them, grasping them, gathering them, hauling them in like fish, her arms the net, and in her embrace the stranger once again became whole.

Pete glared at her.

She stared back, confused, concerned, at sea, with no mast, no oars, no anchor.

"What is it?" he demanded.

"I don't know! It broke in. It's not my fault!"

"You had to go hug it, though, didn't you? You had to do *that*." Pete slammed the shower on, not bothering to draw the curtain; water splattered over them both. Over all three of them. He took off his boots very carefully, cursing the blood slicking his fingers, then stripped off his t-shirt and sweatpants. He threw them at Lenore's feet. Bloody wet rags. Hurled down, like a challenge. She stared at Pete's clothes, trying to figure out what he wanted her to do with them. He got in the shower and used up all the hot water, every drop of it, all of it gone down the reddened drain or into the air as steam, as he rinsed and rinsed and rinsed the blood away. Even with the door open, the bathroom got very steamy; she was sticking to herself, sticking to her own bloody clothes, sticking to the heavy, warm, trembling stranger in her arms, so Lenore walked out into the hall, blood and drips of sweat shaking off at each step, and then into the living room. Where she couldn't sit down, because if she did she'd stain the sofa, or the chair, or the floor. The floor was getting stained anyway, of course, but she couldn't really see it in the low illumination that penetrated from the hallway. Pete was still in the bathroom, so, as an experiment, she tried setting the other down again. Instantly it broke apart; she scrambled to get all the fragments back in her arms. Shadows against shadow. Stupid not to turn on the lights. She'd gone to her knees to scoop up the bigger pieces before they could shoot off to the bathroom; as long as she was kneeling, Lenore figured she might as well sit. So she sat, on the bare wood, not the rug, holding the stranger. "Why?" she whispered to it. "Why?"

She heard Pete go into the bedroom. She heard him getting dressed. She heard him pulling the suitcases out from under the bed. They'd talked about a trip to Montreal this summer, or maybe even Newfoundland. Neither of them had ever been to Canada.

"Pete," she said, rocking the stranger gently. It had calmed down some. "Pete." He didn't answer her. She heard drawers opening, closing. The closet. She was bleeding all over; the first wounds were clotting, but the fresher ones were raw and open. A big cut on her chin dripped steadily on the other's poor bristly back. If they sat together like this much longer, they'd be glued to each other. "Pete, I need you to help me."

When he came out of the bedroom, he was fully dressed, gauze wrapped around and around his hands, big square band-aids stuck all over his face. Under his clothes, Lenore imagined, were yards of more gauze, the whole big roll, and all the rest of the adhesive bandages. Though he was carrying both suitcases, hers and his, Lenore said again, "Pete, I need your help."

It was beginning to get light outside.

All she wanted him to do was stand by the bedroom door. She would get up (if she could get up; no, she would get up, because she had to get up) and walk to the threshold, perhaps take one step over the threshold. She would gently break the crusted tendrils of dried blood gluing her to the other. She would toss it, quickly but with care, onto the bed, and jump backwards. Pete would shut the door. That's all he had to do, shut the door. She'd clean herself up, even though there was no more hot water. She'd bandage herself, somehow. Paper towels, maybe. Toilet paper, if she had to. It didn't matter. In the bedroom, the other would break apart, but alone, safe, given time, perhaps it would calm down and recollect itself on its own. All Pete had to do was close the door for her.

Lenore began to explain her plan, but he cut her off. "This is your mess," he said. "You deal with it."

"Pete. Pete. It broke in. It broke the *window*. It came by *itself*."

"You had to go and touch it, though, didn't you? You had to go hug it." A sneer. His tone froze Lenore's heart. She hadn't thought it could freeze any further, she'd been existing at sub-zero for so long.

He couldn't blame her for this, he couldn't, and yet he did.

The other on her lap had not reacted to Pete's reappearance. It was snuggling against her, nuzzling, almost all the way asleep. She was still holding it close, holding it tight. She thought about releasing her hold. Letting it go and not gathering it up again.

Pete walked to the door, a suitcase in each hand, new blood already spotting the swathes of gauze; his gait was heavy, angry, but in his eyes she glimpsed something like… satisfaction.

She would not ask him where he was going. She knew better than to ask if he were coming back.

He had to put the suitcases down in order to open the apartment door. He did not bother to close it again behind him.

Lenore sat on the floor with the other in her lap. Around her, the room grew lighter, objects and obstacles more clearly defined, as day came on. The newcomer slept. Lenore shifted her weight slightly, and felt a dozen, two dozen, cuts open. She was going to have to stand up and shut the door. She was going to have to sweep the bathroom floor. She was going to have to clean just about everything in the apartment. There was no one else to do those things. She held the newcomer, the other, the visitor, the stranger, murmuring to it wordlessly. Arms aching with weariness as well as wounds, Lenore wondered when it would let her go.

WAITING FOR THE FIRE

❧

DENISE FOUND WORK SOMETIMES. ELCY HAD STOPPED looking. Denise bitched about Elcy hanging around the apartment all day and not kicking in on the bills, but it wasn't like Denise was even paying the rent. The last time the landlady had seen any money had been a couple of months ago, and that was only because she'd caught Denise on the avenue between the check-cashing place and the liquor store. Honked her horn at her, Denise said, leaned on it until everybody on the street turned around. So Denise had to walk over to the landlady's car and make nice. The landlady had gotten a couple hundred out of her, but that hadn't stopped the registered letters.

"You're going to drink yourself to death," Elcy said.

"I work, I got a right to relax. You don't do shit."

I get through twenty-four hours, each and every day, Elcy thought. Each and every day, one minute at a time.

"You could clean up once in a while." Denise was on the couch, stretched out full-length.

Right. A week or so back, Elcy'd come home to find the door broken in. Thought they'd been robbed. Thought, good thing I wasn't here when the bastards found out there wasn't anything to steal, cause they coulda gotten mad. Thought, that was a good idea to go for a walk. Half a hour, go outside, see people, maybe say hello to someone, maybe pet a dog. She'd walked to the edge of Adams Park and back, and hadn't spoken to anyone, but still. Anyway, came to discover all that'd happened was Denise'd lost her keys, and kicked the door in.

What did Denise want her to do, sweep the floor? They didn't even have a broom.

"We should get out of here," Elcy said. "Out of this town. Go to Ithaca, or some place like that."

Denise drank a beer. "You and your Ithaca. You go, you want to so much."

Denise had long black hair she kept in a ponytail, bound with a green rubber band. Always a green rubber band. Couldn't be any other color.

"There's nothing here," Elcy said.

"There's nothing anywhere."

"I used to make you happy," Elcy said.

Denise drank another beer.

"You'd miss me if I left. Who would you talk to when you had bad dreams?"

"I never remember my dreams."

That was complete bullshit. Denise woke up shaking three, four times a month. Crying, too, sometimes. Elcy got mad. "Fine," she said. "Okay. You want me to go? I'm going. You see how you like your life without me."

"Like there'll be any difference. Go, stay, nothing'll change."

Elcy couldn't even slam the door, because the damn thing would have fallen off its hinges.

She spent the night in Adams Park. And all the next day. And all the next night. Once she thought she heard Denise calling for her, and started to jump up, and found herself flailing around in the dead leaves and wind-blown garbage behind the locked-up equipment shed on the edge of the soccer field. She'd been asleep; she'd dreamed it.

Stay or go. Nothing changed.

Nobody talked to her. She didn't talk to anybody. A woman with a big hat walked up and down the bike path, hexing the squirrels. "Eat metal," she chanted. "Eat metal and choke. Eat metal and rust."

Denise was not going to come looking for her. Elcy could dream all she wanted, but reality was reality.

She went back to the apartment. Twenty-four hours in every day. That didn't change, no matter where you were.

And it was cold in the park, and there were bugs, and too many people.

The door was still broken, of course. Denise hadn't even bothered to stick a chair under the knob. Nothing to steal, and besides, the only people likely to drop by were a couple of the landlady's athletic grandchildren, baseball bats in hand. Denise would probably grunt and offer them beers.

The lights were off. They'd been on when Elcy had walked out. Maybe the electric company had caught up with them.

Maybe Denise wasn't home.

Maybe Denise had gone, too. Elcy knew that when Denise left, it wouldn't be in the half-assed way she'd done it, getting only as far as the park, hiding in bushes and behind sheds like some little kid. And when Denise walked out, she wouldn't slink back two days later. Denise would leave, and then, if they ran into each other months later, years later, Denise might blink at her. At most nod. Act like Elcy was someone she'd known ages ago, but not well. Like from high school. Somebody she'd sat through Algebra 1 with. That wasn't how they'd started, but it was the way they'd ended up.

Elcy stood in the dark, listening. She thought she heard breathing. She felt for the light switch on the wall. She definitely heard breathing. Denise passed out on the couch, she thought. That's what I'm hearing. She found the light switch, and pushed it. The electric company hadn't cut the juice on them. The light came on.

Denise was on the couch, but not passed out. Not even sleeping. Her eyes were open. The light must have hurt her, but she didn't turn her head. There weren't any empty bottles on the floor next to the couch.

"What is it?" Elcy asked.

After a moment, Denise said, "What did you see out there?"

Out there? "Nothing. I mean—" Confused, Elcy closed the broken door. "What do you mean? I was in the park."

"Go look," Denise said. She didn't move.

"Look at what? Where?"

"In the kitchen."

The kitchen was only a few feet away. It was where the sink and the refrigerator was. There was nothing else there. They didn't even have a stove. There hadn't been a stove when they moved in. Take it or leave it, the landlady had said. But they still called it the kitchen.

"What's in the kitchen?"

Denise was done talking. She closed her eyes.

Elcy could still hear something, in addition to Denise's breathing. Some other kind of breathing, some different sort of in, pause, out, crackly type of sound. She walked toward the kitchen, looking at Denise as she passed her. It wasn't like Denise to keep her eyes closed that way. But maybe the light was bothering her.

Elcy saw it as soon as she turned to face the sink. Denise put a candle on the floor, she thought. That's strange. But it wasn't a candle. They didn't have any candles, and anyway, there was no tall thin taper, no squat cylinder, no nothing. There was only a flame. It was the flame that was breathing.

The flame grew out of the floor. It was white. It didn't smell of anything, not gas, not burning wood, not hot wax. There was no wick, there was no wax, there was no wood. There was only the flame, white, steady in its respirations, a foot high, almost a foot wide. The floor around it was not scorched or charred. The floor around it was gone. As she watched, more of the floor disappeared. There was no smoke. There was no heat. There was the flame, growing. And the floor, vanishing.

Elcy sat down, on the filthy kitchen floor. The flame wasn't growing quickly, but it was growing. The matter around it wasn't vanishing quickly, but it was vanishing.

Well, she thought. She felt calm. What did you see outside, Denise had asked. Elcy had seen nothing like this outside. It could be that she hadn't noticed. It could be that this was only for them.

God, how stupid was it to think that. To imagine they were special. They used to be something, but they weren't anything anymore, not alone, and not together. And even when they'd been together, they hadn't been anything extraordinary. A special end for a couple of nothings? Yeah, right.

The thought hadn't even crossed Denise's mind. She'd expected Elcy to say, yeah, there are these weird flames all over the place, burning everything up, without any smoke or smell or heat.

But Elcy hadn't seen them. So she could pretend, for a while at least, that this fire was theirs alone. So what if pretending was stupid. It didn't hurt anyone.

The flame was growing. The flame came from somewhere that wasn't here. The flame breathed, and expanded.

In a minute, she would get up and go sit with Denise. Sit on the floor next to the couch, lean her head against the armrest. Maybe Denise would let her hold her hand.

There was nothing to worry about anymore.

There was nothing to wish for anymore.

Elcy sat on the kitchen floor and let herself enjoy the relief. Without wanting to, without realizing that she was going to, she started to laugh.

The flame breathed in and out. It grew.

After a while, on the couch, Denise began laughing, too.

The Jaculi

WHEN THE JACULI FIRST ARRIVED IN THE NEIGHBORHOOD, we gave them a lot of grief. This was mainly due to so many of us being all ignorant and whatnot. And on top of that, as if plain old natural human ignorance wasn't enough, a lot of folks were already on edge. The night the jaculi started jumping, we were sweating through our third blackout that July.

From our rooftops, from our windows, from the street corners where we sat on hot cement and fanned ourselves under the dead traffic lights, we could see the glow of lit-up high-rises and office buildings to the north. The first blackout had affected the whole city, and went on for fifteen hours. Damn, they'd nearly run out of candles up north. All their ice cubes had melted, yeah, and D-cell batteries had gone for ten bucks a pop. Meanwhile, down here, precious few folk had had candles or D-cells, or anywhere to buy them, in the first place. After the power came back on, the mayor got hit with a lot of flak from the people who count. We all watched him standing in front of a dozen TV cameras, him wiping his bald head and vowing it would never happen again. So the second and third blackouts were just for us, a big old raised middle finger from the power company and city hall together, aimed at our concrete triangle below Blue Street. Maybe they all forgot that there were people living down here, that it wasn't all warehouses and meatpacking plants and twenty-four-seven sweatshops churning out t-shirts and ball caps and cut-rate bridal gowns. Maybe they forgot it was a neighborhood crammed with old folks and children.

It was hot. It was dark. And it was the third time in two damn weeks. Even the little kids had quit thinking it was fun camping out on the project roofs and eating jelly sandwiches by candlelight.

Down here below Blue Street, we've got three borders. To the southwest is the river. This is our hypotenuse, the longest side of our triangle. The water is flat, the current sluggish; the river is gray on top, black below. Anyone who eats a fish pulled out of that muck is a fool to himself, but there are plenty of fools in the world, and on summer days you can always see a bunch of tough guys with poles pulling butt-ugly floppy things out of the water. To the north, a highway cuts the neighborhood off from the rest of the city. Our elders, those seniors who haven't completely locked themselves away behind the barricades of their subsidized old-people-jails, those who come out to tell stories sometimes, they talk about the days before the highway was cut through like it was another world, the dreamtime when we were all one city. To the east are the deadlands, empty blocks, the buildings abandoned, or burnt down, or razed, years ago, and never rebuilt. Of course people live there, too. People and other things. Those of us with jobs and families and lives try to stay out of the deadlands. Night, day, makes no matter. We stay out. But the first jaculi that bounded in arrived from the east, and some hotheads, some guys and some women with no damn sense, jumped up and started chasing them, chasing the darting jaculi back to the east. After they'd stopped screaming, that is, after the heroes made sure they hadn't all-the-way shit their shorts. Then they started running after our visitors, with the rest of us hollering after them to stop, stop running, east, east, goddamn idiots, that way is east!

They came back, sort of sheepish. Except for one woman, a punked-out girl who'd moved to the neighborhood the fall before, told everyone she was going to college. If she was, it must've been some on-line thing, because no one ever saw her on the street in the daylight. Well, no one ever saw her anywhere after the night of the third blackout. She ran east, whooping, swinging her serious survive-the-bomb camo-colored flashlight like a club. She ran too far.

The jaculi jumped, jumped, jumped. It looked like there were millions of them, sure, but that was because they moved so fast, darted so swiftly, leapt with such amazing, neck-whipping celerity. We saw the same one a dozen times in a minute, and thought we were seeing twelve separate entities.

Flying snakes, we thought. Flying snakes as long and as thick around as the arms of roid-rushing gymrats. Oh, the screaming; folks screamed for damned-near-ever, it seemed like, like those car alarms that break the night over and over and over again, then quit for a second, exactly long enough for you to heave a sigh of relief, but just as the ringing in your ears is about to fade, kick up once more, the eternal urban music box. The people were screaming exactly like that.

But, to be fair, the jaculi were pretty alarming. Flying serpents are bad enough (it took some of us quite a while to be convinced that the jaculi weren't actually flying, but leaping and jumping, not merely with astounding swiftness, but with remarkable range—on the corner where our group had planned to pass the long, sweaty night, we saw jaculi bound from our side of the street to the top of the two-story car-detailing place on the other side in one lightning leap; it surely looked like flight), but their faces, when one stopped still for the second it took to get a fair look in the light of wavering candles and shaking flashlights, chilled the hearts of even the most level-headed among us. The jaculi had heads the size of softballs, which was one big fat clue we weren't dealing with some mass escape from a secret herpetarium here. Second clue: the jaculi were beaked, with the strong, curved, wicked beaks of raptors. Third: their eyes were as big and round and brown as the eyes of cows, though much steelier.

Mothers pulled their kids off the roofs and hustled them into the oven-heat of airless apartments. Old folks who hadn't ventured outside in the first place shut their windows and pulled their blinds and huddled in the dark, hoping that, once more, being invisible would spare them. Men who'd already had a few beers to cool off, and women with no sense, dashed into their homes and emerged with weapons, pretty silver pistols and big black gangster pieces, swords bought rusty and dull from the Elista Thrift Shop, sheathless hunting knives bought drunk at three in the morning off an exuberant infomercial, nunchucks, fire axes that hadn't struck a lick in fifty years, spray cans of ninety-nine-cent store cockroach killer, and more than one home-rigged Taser. The neighborhood warriors, the ones who always met a smirk with a fist.

Meanwhile the jaculi leapt and darted, jumped and almost-flew. Zipping over our heads, landing on balconies, landing on ledges, landing on top of telephone poles and the long curved arms of traffic lights. The jaculi would pause a moment, then coil and spring again. They seemed restless to us, those of us still watching them instead of chasing them, those of us whose bodies no longer responded to stimulus with immediate flight or fight, or perhaps never had. The jaculi had come from somewhere, maybe from the deadlands to the east, maybe not, but they had come for a reason. They were searching. Hunting.

Our warriors pursued, and hollered, and threw things, and shot at the jaculi. We gave the jaculi some damn hard grief, that first night. We gave ourselves more. Folks with alcohol-impaired aim and no sense shooting pistols and semis and crossbows into the air. Imagine. It was a lucky thing the mothers had taken the kids inside, and that most of the old folks were still sharp enough to stay away from the windows after they'd closed them and drawn the blinds. As it was, some folks on the street got hit by bullets on their way down, a lot of glass was smashed, many walls punctured, telephone poles pocked and chewed, wires snapped. Once the blood started to flow, some women got their sense back and set after the men they had a claim on to haul them back from idiocy, and the shouts went up for medics.

That helped some more folks got their sense back and start transporting the really hurt to a central location, the intersection of Spinet and Summit, where there was a big old parking lot out in front of the convenience store that had gone out of business in April. And more folks brought their flashlights and candles and, no kidding, hurricane lamps and set them up so the medics would be able to see what they were doing and who was bleeding from where and how serious it was. And some folks broke into the back of the boarded-up convenience store just in case there was anything left in there, but there wasn't.

Meanwhile the jaculi kept jumping.

And the parking lot was filling up with moaning and cursing and bleeding folks, and a few who weren't moaning or cursing or even moving at all. Medics, medics, people were hollering, nobody being dumb enough to expect a doctor, but many hoping there was an LPN somewhere, an EMT maybe, or at least someone who'd passed high-school first aid.

We lost a few people that night, due to our being ignorant and all. First, the wanna-be punk girl who ran into the east too far, then a couple more, from bullets. We might have lost more, we might have lost a whole lot before the night was over, especially older folks and little kids, locked up in stifling, two-hundred degree rooms out of fear.

The jaculi kept on jumping. Agitated, searching, seeking. Once in a while one of them let out a sort of cheep. That was the only sound we ever heard them make, except for the whoosh of air as they leapt past our heads.

The shooting had stopped. Some of the women had got hold of their men, and some of the men had got hold of their own selves, and though folks still cried out when a jaculus sprang over them, still pointed and cursed, with real bleeding going on in the parking lot and real death hovering, folks started to focus on what was likely to happen once daylight arrived, or power was restored, whichever came first. A few folk sort of surreptitiously slipped off to the southwest. The river received a number of offerings that night, we came to believe, most of them metal, both the compact, shiny, silvery type and the mean matte black sort.

But we still didn't know what to do about the wounded, except drip water on their heads and try to blot up the blood with paper towels, and the jaculi were still darting all over the place, and though we could tell now that there weren't as many of them as we'd first thought, their speed and their unceasing motion, not to mention their snake bodies and eagle beaks and bovine eyes, had all of us very, very nervous. A lot of us spent more time flinching and trying to look out of the corners of our eyes in all possible directions just in case one of the jaculi took the notion to dart at us than paying close attention to the hurt people lying on the hot asphalt of the parking lot.

We might have lost a lot more than we did. It really could have been a lot worse. For a while there, for about half an hour after the shooting mostly stopped (some folks never did get their sense back that night; some folks got their stupid fixed down deep in the middle of their bones), it looked like it was going to be.

Then the grandmothers came.

How they got themselves all organized the way they did we never managed to figure out. Sure, some folks had cell phones, and some of the cell phones were working that night. Maybe it was that, one grandma with a teenage grandbaby in the house who knew another grandma with a great-niece in the house, who knew another... linking up like a chain. Maybe they all knew each other already; none of us would have put that past them. They all arrived together, all grim and prepared, carrying supplies, and they all worked together like a veteran team, not talking to each other very much, just pointing and nodding and passing bandages and scissors, sharing gauze, helping each other hold folks down while another grandmother did her work, trading drugs with no argument or fuss. They didn't talk much to the rest of us, either, just did their work with their lips pursed and their shoulders bent and sad, like they'd seen all this before and were grieving over seeing it again, but the work had to be done, and they were going to by-damn do it.

Grandma, over here. Grandma, please, look at my sister. Grandma, this guy's passed out, help. That's what we said, softly, most of us, no screaming, no yelling, most of us acting with sense, and after a while grandma started sounding too familiar, not respectful enough, and we switched to grandmother.

Not all of the grandmothers were women. There was a fair sprinkling of men among them. It was one of the men, a bald guy with a long fringe of white hair, who between pulling slivers of glass out of a woman's face with tweezers and splinting a kid's leg, looked up and told us what the jaculi were. Jaculi, plural, jaculus, singular, from the Latin jacere, to throw or cast, named so from their darting motions. Imaginary creatures found in a couple old books that had passed for science texts a few hundred years ago.

Imaginary? They don't look so imaginary, grandmother, one person said, his voice low and respectful.

The old guy looked up again, and nodded. *Not so imaginary any more,* he agreed. Then he went back to wrapping bandages around the splint.

Not all the grandmothers were old. There was a fair sprinkling of younger women among them. It was one of these, an iron-haired woman in a photographer's vest, every pocket of which was bulging with pill bottles and boxes and vials, who told us, *Feed them. They're here, so we might as well make friends with them. Feed them.* Then she went back to handing out pills and powders and ointments.

So then, naturally, we were faced with the difficulty of figuring out what imaginary beasts from old Latin books might eat. This wasn't altogether a bad thing, though the discussion turned a bit heated once or twice, because it gave those of us with nothing else to do but stand around and be worried, which was frankly most of us, something to occupy us.

Meanwhile the jaculi jumped, and jumped, and jumped. But they must've been getting some tired themselves, because they were pausing more, resting more; it seemed like they were catching their wind before leaping again. This allowed those of us who wanted to look the chance to get in a good glance or two.

Look at their eyes, someone said.

Damn, those beaks, someone else said softly.

They're sort of beautiful, said another of us.

In the end, we decided that the jaculi most likely were meat-eaters, given the shape of their beaks and the fact that everything below their necks was definitely snake, and none of the snakes we could think of were vegetarians. The next argument arose over whether the jaculi were live-prey feeders or carrion eaters. This debate was starting to turn heated, too, when one of us threw up her hands in disgust and said the hell with it, the meat in her freezer was spoiled anyway, since she hadn't thrown it out after the second blackout, like you were supposed to, but now after another one she sure as shit wasn't going to eat it herself, so why not try it and see. She stomped off, muttering to herself, casting dark glances at the rooftops, the telephone poles, the long arms of the traffic lights.

If we feed them they'll never go away, someone objected. *Like, you know, stray cats, or rats, or pigeons. And damn, but we got enough stray cats and rats and pigeons around here, don't we? Do we really need flying snakes, too?*

So that was the third argument, but the grandmother had said to feed them, so that argument was pretty well settled by the time our volunteer came hauling a shopping bag with a few cling-wrapped chunks of nearly-thawed hamburger meat and a styrofoam tray of chicken legs.

It turned out that the jaculi loved nearly-thawed chunks of gray hamburger and drippy raw chicken legs. They cheeped when they saw our volunteer unwrap the contents of her freezer and toss the gloppy bits into the middle of the street. It was clear to all of us that these were cheeps of eagerness, and of joy. Then whoosh, whoosh, whoosh, they descended, swarming the food like starving things.

See, what did I tell you? Just like pigeons, said the one who'd lost that argument. He was still disgruntled. *Remember, what goes in's gotta come out. I bet they poop like Rottweilers, these things.*

Shut up, we told him gently.

The jaculi ate quickly, but neatly. In under a minute, all the scraps of hamburger and the chicken legs had disappeared.

The jaculi cheeped again. They looked at us hopefully.

See, I told you. Just like cats. Now they'll never—

Shut up, we reminded him.

At that point, the grandmothers told us to take it up the block and let them work in peace, so we did. We moved our gathering back to the intersection of Summit and Spinet. The shooting and shouting and acting all stupid had died away by now. Windows were open again, and folks were leaning out, a little nervously, wiping their faces, fanning themselves. A few mothers had brought their kids back to the rooftops. As we walked to Spinet and Summit, we waved at these cautious, brave folks encouragingly. In the end, we didn't lose anyone because they'd feared too much and locked themselves in the heat and the airlessness too long. Folks who got their nerve back went to check on those who hadn't and convinced them to open the windows, come out for a breath of cooler air.

Those of us who had stocked-up freezers and fridges sacrificed their contents. For the rest of the night, we fed the jaculi. It was easy to see, when they were all together, that there really were much fewer of them than it had first appeared. Not hundreds, oh no. Certainly not thousands, the way some of the folks who lost their sense the earliest were screaming only a couple of hours ago. Maybe four dozen, maybe five, tops.

We discovered, by trial and error, that the jaculi would eat soggy unfrozen waffles, but not soggy, unfrozen peas. They would eat fish sticks, but not crinkle-cut potatoes. Well, not any potatoes, period. They would, some children discovered with glee, eat jelly sandwiches.

The night grew cooler toward dawn, and a slight breeze began to blow, which was a welcome relief, though we all had lived there long enough to know that the heat and the humidity would snap down like a lid as soon as the sun rose. The sky turned gray, and we began to distinguish colors again instead of merely shapes, and one by one people blew out their candles and switched off their flashlights.

The jaculi were not gluttons. They ate until they were satisfied, and then they stopped, and more slowly then, with more effort and less of a whoosh, leapt to many separate high places. There they looped around themselves, coiling as serpents do, ending up beak to tail, and settled down to sleep.

We didn't get the electric back until late in the afternoon of the next day. And what did we see on our TVs as soon as those electronic eyes opened up? What did we hear on our radios when we switched them on? What did we see online when we connected?

Jaculi. Jaculi all over the city, leaping and darting like ours, but not like ours. Frantic, desperate jaculi, hunted from tree to tree and post to post and roof to roof by grim men in uniforms, jaculi caught in nets, broken with clubs, shot, killed. Killed, and killed, and killed. And hysterical people, folks with no sense, screaming and crying that the authorities weren't doing enough, weren't killing the jaculi (not that anyone on the TV knew that jaculi was the name for them) fast enough.

It was heartbreaking. After almost a full day with the jaculi in our neighborhood, most of us had come around to the opinion first expressed by one or two during the long night of the blackout: that the jaculi were beautiful.

Some of us had jobs outside the neighborhood. We didn't go to them that day, or the next. It looked like everybody north of us was busy going crazy, and we decided to leave them to it. We all went about our lives, fixed up stuff that had been broken during the power outage and our own, smaller, craziness at that time. We visited the grandmothers, made sure they all had working fans and ice in their freezers. We kept on taking care of the folks who had been hurt. We decided what to do about the three individuals who'd died in the parking lot, two of whom had no families willing to claim them, and one who did. We thought about the punk girl who'd disappeared in the deadlands to the east. There wasn't anything we could do about that, but we thought about her. We didn't forget her. We went on, as we always did, in our triangle below Blue Street.

The one thing we didn't do was feed our jaculi. We didn't have to.

As it turned out, they were very skillful hunters. As soon as they got themselves acclimatized, which basically happened once they'd slept off the freezer-scrap meal we'd fed them, they began to fend for themselves.

Nobody mourned the loss of the rats, and only a few protested the culling of the pigeons. Rather more of us got upset at the lowered population of stray cats, and there was talk of mounting rescue operations to trap the cats in humane cages and get them adopted, but we'd had those discussions before, and just like always, nothing came of it this time, either. In the end people accepted that this was the way nature worked. Some ate, and some got eaten.

The jaculi have been with us for months now. They have built nests, and some folks claim they have seen eggs in those nests. This is good news, most of us think. In the rest of the city, the jaculi have grown rare. A sighting or two is reported every couple of weeks, and whenever one is spotted, no effort seems to be spared to hunt it down, discover where it's been hiding, and kill it.

Now winter is coming, and we wonder if the eggs will hatch before then. We wonder if the jaculi will need our help to feed the little ones, or if they will be able to manage on their own even when snow covers the sidewalks and the pigeons and cats are harder to spot. We wonder, some of us, if the jaculi will hibernate. This is such a point of interest that considerable sums have been wagered on it. We wonder if the jaculi can be domesticated. If, for example, a young one fell out of its nest, and one of us took it home, might we tame it and raise it and have it love us?

We wonder a lot of things. That's the way folks down here have always been, full of questions and wonderments and debates. But mostly we are glad that the beautiful jaculi are with us now. We are sorry for acting like ignorant fools when they first came, and we are glad that they have forgiven us. We hope they stay. Most of all, we are glad that we live in this small neighborhood below Blue Street, and not in one of the soulless ones to the north, where the streets are clean and the avenues all have trees, where people work in buildings tall enough to poke the clouds, and spend all their money on cars and clothes and exercise equipment, and pay for grim men in sharp uniforms to kill every new thing that appears in the world.

SOFT CHILD

SHE KNEW INSTANTLY WHO IT WAS.

He banged on the door, rapid-fire knocks loud as gunshots, heedless of the hour—dragging her head up from the pillow, Candela squinted at the alarm clock... 3:57 in the morning—heedless of the neighbors. Though it had been five years, almost, since he'd left her, and three years since she'd seen him last, a glimpse in a parking lot that had troubled her dreams for days, as she broke out of sleep, her heart racing like a piston, Candela knew: Tommy.

Son of a bitch, she thought, flinging herself out of bed. Stormed to the door in her t-shirt and sweatsocks. Didn't switch on the light. Candela had lived in the same apartment for twenty years; she could navigate its two narrow rooms and kitchenette blindfolded and with her hands jammed into oven mitts. She was going to blast him, she was going to let him have it like no one ever had laid into anyone before; a stream of invective rose up in her throat. She barely kept it under control as she threw the locks back. No point cursing before she got the door open. She wanted to do it to his face. *In* his face.

Three fifty-seven in the blessed morning—

She flung the door wide. Only afterwards did she think, *Should have looked through the peephole, that's what the damn thing's for.* But no, that would have meant using her head. The first blistering word was poised to launch itself off her tongue when she saw that Tommy was carrying his son.

It was like a punch in the stomach. The air whooshed out of her.

The only light in the hallway came from the forty-watt dangling from the cracked ceramic fixture above the landing. Tommy's face was half in shadow, but she saw the strain in it. My god, she thought suddenly, he looks old. I was the gray-haired one, I was the cradle-robber, we used to joke about this back when it was still funny, and now he looks older than me.

He also looked rather ashamed of himself, which was something new. After five years, his first words to her were, "It's four in the morning."

"I know," she said. She wanted to hit him, she wanted to hug him... Tommy's face was etched with desperation. Suddenly she felt very cold.

He gazed at her for a moment, then dropped his eyes; he shifted the child's weight in his arms. Candela deliberately did not look at the boy. She said, surprising herself, "I guess you want to come in."

"Yeah."

"Come in, then."

And it was easy, then, to step back from the door, to turn on the lights, to usher him in, to nod him toward the lumpy loveseat, to start thinking about coffee even though it was four in the morning, to wonder where'd she stashed that gift bottle of brandy—even though it was four in the morning—but it was not easy to look at the little boy.

"I don't believe you still live in this dump. You know the front door's still broken? Anybody could get into the building."

"Like you?"

Tommy collapsed on the loveseat, letting out a sigh of exhaustion before arranging the child's limbs more comfortably in his lap—legs here, together, arms here... Something odd about that. The boy was not asleep; big brown eyes stared at her from under a mop of tousled brown hair. He looked about three years old, but Candela was notoriously bad at judging children's ages. The child's head lay against Tommy's shoulder. His jaw hung loose, a string of dribble connecting his lower lip to his collarbone. His limbs hung loosely, too. Floppy, like a rag doll.

"His name's Lester."

Candela raised an eyebrow.

Tommy sighed again. "His mother's idea." Then he bit his lip, and looked away.

Once, they had sat together for hours in this very room, sometimes talking, other times not needing to talk. Once, Tommy had sat cross-legged on that loveseat, painstakingly decorating a pair of boots for her. Now he couldn't look her in the face.

Candela shivered. Maybe I should put some clothes on, she thought. But she had the feeling that if she left Tommy, even for a moment, when she returned he would be gone.

"She doesn't know I'm here," he said. "Lester's mother."

The boy did not change his slack-jawed expression at the mention of his name. He didn't even blink.

She looked at Tommy, and part of her thought: there are no years. The other part thought, I don't want to know, I really don't. "What do you want?" she said, and if it came out harshly, then that's how it came out.

He swallowed, licked his lip, and swallowed again. "I need your help."

She was still standing; she'd been standing all along, afraid to sit down, as if that would be too cozy, too intimate. Or maybe she stayed on her feet to keep some psychological advantage. As long as I'm looking down on him, I'm in control.

Candela sat on the cracked-leather hassock, tugging her t-shirt down over her knees. "Go on."

"I offended the Rat King," Tommy said, "and he stole Lester's bones. Please, could you get them back?"

Once upon a time they had picnicked in the park every sunny weekend; once upon a time they had raced their bicycles down the lake path and she had consistently beaten him; once upon a time he had cashed out some savings bonds to buy her a drum; and once upon a time they had fought viciously over the question of children, and he had left her.

"Rat King?" she said, in disbelief.

"The King of the Rats."

"There's no such thing. That's a… a story. A folktale."

"Really," he said, and glanced at her from under his brows. *Don't bullshit me. I know, and you know, and I know you know.*

The King of the Rats? Candela shook her head. Outside the narrow window of her front room, the sky was still pitch black. She had the feeling sunrise was going to be a long time coming. "Tell me what happened," she said.

"I can't believe you still live here," he said.

"I like it." And lucky for you I do, or how else would you have found me? It was not as if they had stayed in touch. That time she'd glimpsed him in the parking lot, she'd immediately turned and taken a quick step to the side, concealing herself behind a big white van, afraid he'd say hello, afraid he'd want to do the polite thing and introduce her to the woman he was with.

"You could do better."

"Tell me what happened."

"I'll show you," he said, and began to undress the boy.

It was beginning to dawn on her now that all of this was in the nature of being a professional consultation.

"When did this happen?"

"A month ago."

"All at once, or gradually?"

"All at once." He glanced at her again, fingers busy with buttons. "His mother's taken him to doctors, of course. They say a whole lot of different things."

Well, they would. Outside, a garbage truck rumbled by. A few blocks away, men shouted, glass shattered. The sounds of the city stirring in its sleep.

Lester wore a diaper. Tommy, following Candela's gaze, swallowed painfully. In a soft voice, he said, "Yeah. We weren't using them any more, before this happened. Lester's a big boy." He touched the boy's head. "Aren't you, kid?"

Lester lay draped across Tommy's lap, his head now supported in the crook of his father's elbow. Rising from the hassock, Candela approached reluctantly. I'm too old for this, just last week I dreamed I'd taken my drum to the river... She rubbed her eyes and steeled her heart. "How old is he?"

"He'll be five in September."

Older than she'd thought. The boy's whole body was limp, muscles slack. Picking up one of Lester's hands, she closed the little fingers into a fist; as soon as she released it, the fingers fell open. She picked up a foot and ran a fingernail up its sole from heel to toes. No reaction. "Does he talk?"

Tommy paused. "He did."

"Until a month ago."

"Yeah."

Candela gazed down at the boy's face. Lester's eyes were open, as wide open as they had been all along. Big and brown and liquid; those eyes would break girls' hearts one day, she thought. "He sees, he understands, he knows," Candela said quietly, and Tommy's fingers tightened on his son.

"Can you help him?"

"What do they tell you, the doctors?"

He grimaced. "One says curse, another says changeling. A lot of nonsense. One... one said forget this child, go have another one." He stroked the boy's hair. "My wife cries every night. So do I."

"He doesn't, though. Does he? Lester."

"No. He is very quiet."

Candela straightened up. "All right, Tommy. What did you do?"

"Can I put his clothes back on?"

SOFT CHILD

You didn't have to take them off in the first place. "Sure."

"My fault," he said softly. "I haven't told my wife. It was a night, like this one, everything dark, everything quiet. I went into Lester's room. When you have children you check on them, this is normal." He stopped. "I have to tell you everything, don't I?"

Candela lowered herself to the hassock again. "Why did you come here, Tommy?"

"Because I know you go into and out of the animal world." He was tugging on Lester's socks, not looking at her as he spoke. Once he had called her Bear, once he had called her Hawk, once he had called her Vixen, teasingly... affectionately, he said. She had told him not to, and eventually he had stopped. "All right. In this building you have rats. Don't say you don't, I remember. In my building, it's the same. But we have a treaty with the King."

"There is no King of the Rats," she said again. "That's a story. No one king of all the rats, anyway. This is a condo?"

"Co-op. Anyway," he glanced at her, "we're at peace. Or we were. No traps, no poison—no chewing up our Persian rugs, no turds in the corners. Compromise, yeah?"

"I get it."

"So I went into Lester's room, and maybe I'd had too much to drink. Okay, I'd been drinking all day, and I fell asleep, and when I woke up I was still drunk, you know what I mean?"

"Where was your wife?"

"Conference in Florida. Don't look at me like that, I know. I wasn't being responsible. But it had just been a horrible week, you know? One damn thing after another... and I needed to relax, get out of my brain for a while..." He trailed off. "I'm on the wagon now."

"You went into Lester's room." If he wanted sympathy, he could look in the dictionary between shit and syphilis, she thought.

"A rat was sitting on his chest." Tommy's voice shook. "A big monster rat, gray as iron and as fat as a housecat. I almost passed out. This big thick naked tail wrapped around Lester's wrist, and the rat staring into his face, eye to eye, you know? And his mouth... the rat's mouth was touching Lester's mouth. It looked like they were kissing."

"Breathing each other's breath," she said.

He looked up quickly. "I killed it. Monica had this tall cut-glass vase on a table in the hall. Heavy. I grabbed it and batted the thing off Lester's chest with it. It hit the floor and it must've been stunned for a second, because it just lay there, and I stomped on it, and hit it with the vase. A lot. I hit it until the vase broke. There was a lot of blood."

Candela steepled her fingers. "What did Lester do?"

"He screamed. For like a minute. And then he stopped."

"And he hasn't said anything since. Or moved."

"No." Tommy licked his lip. "I cleaned everything up and went back to bed. Threw the rat down the garbage chute. I thought Lester was all right. After he stopped screaming. I thought he was just scared, you know. And then I thought he'd fallen asleep. So I went to bed and fell asleep again, too—"

Passed out, she thought.

"And sort of dreamed—"

"Sort of dreamed?"

Tommy winced. "The King of the Rats appeared to me, and said, 'That was my grandson you murdered, and now I will take your son's bones.' Stop looking at me like that."

Candela stood up. "There's no such thing as the King of the Rats. Why did you come here tonight?"

"I thought you could help me. I know you can help me." He hugged Lester tightly. The boy had still not blinked once that Candela could tell.

"Did you tell your wife what happened?"

"No. I haven't told anyone. Except you, just now."

And that was it, Candela thought. He came here to keep his secret untold, to keep his guilt hidden. She went and stood by the front room's narrow window, looking out at the dark for a few moments. "They would have been brothers," she said.

"No. Never. It's disgusting. This is my son. Brother to a rat?"

"You prefer him like this?"

Tommy was silent, but when she turned around she saw he'd taken out his wallet and spread its contents over the top of the coffee table, green bills fanned out like playing cards. "Help me. Please. Look at him. You don't know what it's like, when your child is suffering. It's like my heart's been ripped to pieces. Okay, I did something wrong, but Lester didn't. It's not his fault, is it? He doesn't deserve this. Help him, please."

"How long were we together?" Candela asked tightly. "And you throw money down like that, in my house?"

"I figured you could use it."

She studied his face for a minute or two, gazing on him until the pain grew too much and something small but vital broke inside her; her eyes burned, but she would not cry in front of him. I'll live, she told herself, the pain is that of a boil that has burst, and now the poison is draining; but that was a facile wisdom, and though she knew she should believe it, she also knew that she didn't, not yet. Candela lowered her gaze to the boy. Lester stared back at her with his big unblinking brown eyes.

"All right," she said to him. "I'll see what I can do."

She went to her bedroom, shut the door and locked it. In the dark, she opened the closet door; in the dark she undressed; in the dark she put on her travelling clothes, she put on her boots, she put on her hat. She unrolled her rug, she took down her drum. She sat down and prepared, breathing her own breath, chewing her own spit, and when the trail became known, she began to journey.

A spiral in the dark, the path itself darker than the lightless room she sat in, darker than the night that covered the city. The black trail twisted and curled like a fleeing snake, a slippery ribbon continuously on the verge of disappearing from her view. She forded seven rivers and flew across seven plains, greeted seven friends and seven helpers, but refrained from asking for aid. A show of force would be impolitic; the one she journeyed to legitimately considered itself the offended party.

Over the last river, beyond the last mountain, under the last stone. Candela announced her arrival politely. She'd always found tact to be of great use; therefore she did not come in the shape of a rat, but in her own.

"Greetings, uncle."

The old rat crouched on a pile of human bones, small bones, the bones of a young child, limbs and ribs and fingers and toes, pelvis and vertebrae. Its red eyes blinked at her. Slowly, it extended its long, dry tongue and licked the arm bone before it.

"You lick your grief," she said. "Is it salt?"

"Salt from my tears."

"I will redeem the bones."

The rat blinked again, licked again. "The bones are mine. These bones were those of my second grandson. Now they are those of my slave."

"And of what use is a slave? A grandson is better. You made the child soft."

"And you would have him hard again?" The old rat showed its teeth. "He will always be soft."

"You have not chewed the bones."

"I am savoring their pain."

"Savor mine. It is richer."

The old rat cocked its head. "What do you offer?"

Candela extended the little finger of her left hand.

"That pain is not fresh," the rat observed.

"But it is rich."

"It is small recompense for a grandson."

"The boy will recompense you. He will be your grandson as long as he lives."

"Tell me his name," said the rat, and Candela smiled thinly.

"Name him yourself, for now, and when he is grown you will choose a name together."

"You give him to me?"

"I cannot give what is not mine."

"I want him."

"Then let him grow."

The old rat laughed. This is what it had wanted all along, she thought. Too bad about the dead young one; Tommy was such an idiot.

Disgusting, Tommy'd said. Well, he hadn't thought it that damn disgusting when the two of them had been together, had he?

The old rat inclined its head. Candela knelt before it, holding out her left little finger. She closed her eyes; the old rat bit it off.

The journey back was as long as the journey out, as it ever was; it took no time and it took all time. Opening her eyes, Candela set down her drum. She did not know what time it was; she did not know what day it was. She was very hungry and very thirsty, and her head swam as she got to her feet. The pain in her finger was blunt, but the wound in her heart had not yet scabbed over.

Her bedroom was dark. In the darkness, she undressed, put away her things, and dressed again.

Candela did not expect to find Tommy still in the apartment; she knew he would not have had the patience to wait until she returned, and indeed, the front room was empty. He'd left the money, though, dozens of bills fanned out on the coffee table. Nothing else. She stood looking at the cash for a moment; she counted her heartbeats, and when she reached one hundred she burst out laughing.

She never saw Tommy again, not even in her dreams.

The child, though, she did see again, many years later, when he was almost grown. She was sitting on a park bench when the boy passed her, one among a group of tall teenagers in school blazers and loose khakis. She recognized Lester by the shadow that ambled hip-to-hip with his own, a frisky gray twin in rodent form.

Hiding

It is difficult for a person to vanish within the city. There are too many eye-men and nose-women about, on top of all the professional finders. To really disappear, you have to get yourself past the city boundaries. Go somewhere else.

To become invisible is another matter. Cott and I have been invisible for some time. Most folks our own age are gone, and the eyes of the young slide over us without pause. The middle-aged see us, then look away quickly, so we do not register for more than an instant. And the eye-women and nose-men, those inquisitive, curious sorts forever sniffing and peeping over and into and around other people's business? Not even the old ones find us interesting enough to turn their heads as we go by.

Cott gets angry about it. He's always had a temper. Always been impatient. Don't ever give him something to fix, like a noter with a stuck key. If he can't mend it in five minutes, he'll throw it in the trash. After smashing it against the edge of the kitchen table three or four times, so the screen goes dead. "We'll get a new one. We'll get a new one, all right?"

He hasn't any great patience with people who don't see him, either. Somebody bumps into him on the street and says, "Sorry, didn't see you," Cott rears back like he's been challenged to a duel. And if the person doesn't say anything, jostles him and just keeps going, I have to grab his arm to stop him from taking a swing.

And stores. Oh, dear, stores. If he gets ignored in a shop, there's nothing to do but stand back and let him shout, otherwise he'd just rant at home, and for a lot longer. Yelling at clerks or cashiers or managers doesn't get him any better service, of course, but it makes Cott feel like he's making a point, or shaming them, at least. He's not, of course. They forget about us as soon as we leave.

Myself, I enjoy being invisible. To observe without being observed—there are many small pleasures in that, little moments of amusement and enlightenment. There's even, if I'm honest, a sense of power. I see you, and you don't see me. I hear everything you're saying, and you are oblivious. I know something about you, and you are not aware that I exist. When I would go for a walk, or even to the corner store, without Cott, I'd usually come home smiling. Cott knew that smile. He thought it was perverse. "What did you see this time, teenagers kissing? A drunk puking? Hey, did somebody slip on a squishy dog turd?"

I never try to change people. Never tried to change Cott. I let people be. I wouldn't think of asking him to take a look at the coffee grinder, or the loose light switch. And if I see him pick up a screwdriver with a purposeful expression on his face, I'll distract him if I can, stay out of his way if I can't. So when he rolled his eyes when I came home smiling, I let him be. Didn't argue. Didn't fight.

When I stopped going out by myself, Cott didn't notice for a while.

I enjoyed being invisible, and that's gone now. People look. Some people. But it's only going to get worse. Soon everybody's going to look. Everybody's going to stare. In this city, there are certain things that draw attention. There are certain changes that catch the eye.

It was only after I started making excuses when Cott wanted to go for a walk together, or to the store together, or to a concert on the plaza, which is something that we used to do in the summer, that he caught on.

"This?" he said. "This?" He took my hands in his. That was a loving gesture, and he did it gently, but he was already angry. He's never learned to hide his anger. It is always right there in his eyes.

Hiding is different from being invisible. It is different from vanishing, too.

"Nobody's going to care about this," he said. "We're not living in the old days, for pity's sake. The municipal authorities are not going to come around, lock you up. Come on. I can't believe you're afraid of that." He was growing angrier. "These are modern times!"

I wasn't afraid. He didn't understand that, wouldn't understand it. I wasn't afraid of being treated as dangerous, and I wasn't afraid of the changes, either. These things happen. We all know, living in this city, that they do, and that they can strike anyone. No one thinks it's an evil spell anymore, the way they used to in what Cott calls the old days. (The old days. I was in elementary school when the courts finally caught up with the scientists and declared changers simply another protected minority. So was he.) Most of the time, the changes come when you are young. It was unusual for it to occur at my age. It happened, though. It happened. It didn't bother me that it was happening to me. Not that, in and of itself.

"Your hands are beautiful," Cott said. He was almost shouting. "Your hands are goddamn wonderful!"

It wasn't going to stop with my hands, of course.

Changers live freely now. They go to school, they can apply for any job they want, live anywhere they can afford. Nobody stares at them much in the street.

Not the young ones. Not the ones that have been changers since they were kids, teenagers. People get used to them, and over the years, they become invisible, too, mostly.

Old changers are unusual.

"I'm not afraid," I told Cott. I tried to explain to him that what I felt was… a sort of grief. This didn't make sense to him, so he refused to believe me.

I would have let him be, if he had decided he wanted to stay home, interact with the world through screens and pads, live his life his own way. But when I did it, he called it hiding, and nagged me constantly.

"You won't even go out in the garden!"

"I never liked gardening. You like gardening. So garden."

"Fresh air," he shouted.

"They have these things called windows, you know. They open."

It went on like that, and it went on like that. And my hands, which were silver, began to sparkle, even in a dim room, not only when the sun came through the windows, and my chin split, a cleft of new flesh that was silver, too, but not glittery like the skin on my hands. I discovered that the cleft was a new organ, if that's the right word. Suddenly I could smell water. This was interesting. There were many variations, gradations, to the scent. Scents, really. Many different elements that perhaps were not really odors, but sensations that my mind processed as odors. All this was new, and interesting, and even a little bit enjoyable, and in that scrap of pleasure I found some balm for my grief.

"Stop washing your face. How many times a day are you going to wash your face?"

Cott didn't understand at all. I never let him see me cry. It would only have made him angry, for it would have made him feel helpless, and nothing infuriated him more than that.

And then Ellem Zus vanished, and Cott became intolerable.

Ellem Zus was a little boy who lived up the street, with his parents and his younger sister and an aunt or great-aunt of some sort. He went off to school one morning, a morning like any other, or so his parents said, and never arrived. And then he didn't come home. And then his parents searched his room, before they called in the municipal authorities, and discovered that Ellem had taken some clothes, and a bit of money (and a bit more money, from a box secreted at the very back of the top shelf of one of the kitchen cupboards), and the charms that his aunt or great-aunt had given him, one for each birthday. When the municipal authorities arrived, they sniffed around, conducted their own search, declared *runaway*, and assured Ellem's parents that a team of finders would be put on the case.

"He's eight years old," Cott said, pacing. And pacing. "What eight-year-old runs away?"

"He's eleven," I said. "Probably had an argument with his parents, so he's lying low at a friend's house. The finders will trace him down by morning."

"His folks are besides themselves." Cott had gone over, when the municipal authorities arrived and the commotion started. There's always commotion with the municipal authorities. They love their grand entrances, their mounted scouts, their uniformed scholars, their knights, and their plainclothes Cleaners. They probably would have put on the same show for a lost cat. Cott and I had both worked for the municipal authorities, in different departments. Not so unusual. The municipal authorities employed nearly thirty percent of the workforce of the city, in one capacity or another. I'd always thought the pomp and regalia ridiculous, but that was the way of the city.

"Of course they are. It's natural."

Ellem was a slight boy, small for his age, dark. He used to wave to me when he saw me in the garden. And that was all I knew about him, except for the fact that he was eleven, because I'd heard him win an argument with another child by stating that since he, Ellem, was eleven, and the other kid was ten, Ellem had to be correct. I hadn't caught what the two boys had been disputing, but the other child had said a bad word and given in.

Cott kept pacing.

"Sometimes children run away from a bad situation," I said.

"You don't even know his parents."

This was true.

"You always assume parents are to blame. Just because your parents—" He stopped himself.

He stopped himself, but this time I didn't let him be. "Why are you so upset?"

He knew what I was saying. After so much time together, after so many words spoken, there was rarely any need for long dialogs. Sometimes even a gesture would communicate decades of history. He walked out of the room and went to pace somewhere else.

We'd never had children of our own. Cott had said over and over that he didn't blame me, even though I was so set against it I wouldn't let him discuss it even in hypothetical terms. He said he accepted my decision. But you can accept something to keep the peace, bury it down so deep you can forget about it for years, but certain things don't vanish, ever. And since they're always still there, they can always come back, given the right push, the wrong word.

Cott had wanted children. I had refused. And every time there was a story about a child on the news, a child hurt or killed or kidnapped or lost, he got angry. And, of course, being helpless to do anything about hurt or lost or dead children we didn't know just made his anger hotter.

He knew this one, if only by sight. He knew the parents now, even though neither of them probably remembered the old man who'd walked into their house and listened to one of the Lord Knights of the City asking them questions while the plainclothes Cleaners drifted through the rooms, hunting for traces.

Ellem was not found by nightfall. He was not found the next day, or the day after.

The municipal authorities returned to the house up the block, and departed again.

And Cott started in on me.

"Oh, for the love of plums and sweet tea, will you just give the professionals a chance to do their job."

"You're a professional," he said.

"I'm retired. Remember? We even had a party." Twenty years ago, almost.

"The finders can't locate any signs. The Cleaners and the Sweepers say nothing has been disturbed within the pools of force, or along the conduits of energy. The fountains are quiet. Ellem hasn't been snatched up by some malevolent spell-weaver. He hasn't just run away. Remember the charms he took? He can work them. I talked to the great-aunt. She said the kid had talent. So I think he's using the charms to hide."

"He's eleven. When he runs of out food, runs out of money, or just gets bored, he'll come home." I had a thought, and looked at Cott.

"No," he said. "I talked to the sister. Ellem wasn't a changer."

"You're getting pretty cozy with the family."

"Don't you understand? They're going out of their minds."

You too, I thought. You're making yourself crazy over this, which is in no possible way your business, so you can stop making yourself crazy over me. Good plan. Except you've got to link the two things in order to push that plan forward.

"You want me to look for him."

"You know the castings of concealment."

"You think the finders and the scholars don't?"

"I think the charms the great-aunt gave the boy were old ones, and magic changes just the same as technology does. Maybe none of the people working on the case have any idea how the old charms function."

"Cott."

"Take a walk with me. Just one walk."

"Cott."

"He's a little boy." And the anger was gone from him, even from his eyes, replaced by anguish. Maybe Cott would have made a good father, or maybe he would have made his children crazy, and not in the eccentric, entertaining way. He'd never had a chance to find out. I would have been a terrible parent. Any child of mine, I would have hurt beyond repair, beyond forgiveness. I'd known that since I was ten years old. I'd tried to tell Cott that the pain the children he wanted would suffer counted more, weighed much more, than any satisfaction or pride he might get from being a father. He said he accepted that. He never has.

Of course it wasn't satisfaction or pride that he yearned for. I had used those words because I couldn't use the true one.

"You want me to take a walk with you."

"I bet he's hiding close by."

"I haven't done this for twenty years."

"Are you telling me you've forgotten how?"

No. I hadn't forgotten how.

"Don't tell me fishing for a hiding is too exhausting. Don't tell me you've gotten old." Cott tried to sound like he was teasing, but the pain never left his eyes.

Fishing. Angling. Casting. The words we use for what we do, for what we did, because we have no other words.

No, it wouldn't be too hard, too exhausting. I could smell water now. Tasting a hiding would probably be easy. The air around a charm takes on flavors as well as scents, as well as sensations that can be felt on the skin: warmth, cold, the static tingle of contained power. Perceptible, to those who have studied, who have trained. And he was right about the old charms having a different makeup, different structures, from modern ones.

"I don't want to go outside," I said. "But I will. For you. But I need to tell you something."

"Anything."

"You might not like what we find."

He hadn't expected that. I knew what he thought I was going to say: *you're the biggest nag I've ever known in my life, you never can simply let things be.* That sort of thing, which he'd heard often enough. For a second, he looked surprised. But then he smiled, and said, "I love you."

"I know."

There is hiding in plain sight. For this, the main requirement is making oneself appear perfectly ordinary and unremarkable. There is hiding in complicated sight, which has a sibling relationship to being invisible. You make people not want to see you, or remember you. Then there is the traditional hiding, as in the cellar of an abandoned building, a disused subway tunnel—going underground literally, rather than metaphorically. It's surprising how often people revert to that, to their animal instincts. And then there is the use of charms.

I should have talked to the great-aunt, I thought, as Cott led me out into the street, his arm hooked through mine, I should have found out what sort of charms she'd given the boy as birthday gifts. Generic ones, most likely, and old ones, as Cott had guessed. Perhaps they had been given to her in her own childhood. Old charms may fade, but they might also gather energy as they slept, untouched, for years and decades. If the boy was using them, he must have some talent, but still, he was only eleven. Talent without training was dangerous.

People looked at us. At me, and at Cott because he was with me. My hands were silver and sparkly, and my chin was split. In addition, the day before I had discovered feathers in my hair. People looked, and made remarks to each other, and followed us with their eyes.

We walked several blocks, Cott holding my arm, Cott whispering, "Anything yet? Anything yet?" until I wanted to slap him.

"You're not trying," he said.

I didn't look at him. "I want to go home."

"You said you'd do this. Think of the child. Think of his parents."

I wasn't. I thought of Cott, and how he'd grieved for fifty years over having no children of his own.

"Let's walk north a bit," I said.

There was a tingling under the new flesh of my separated chin. It wasn't a smell, or a taste, but it felt like the precursor of one.

When I was eleven, there were certain things I knew. I knew my parents were wrong when they beat me. And I knew that no one, no family member, no neighbor, no representative of the municipal authorities, would stop them. This was in the old days, as Cott calls them. Things are supposed to be different now.

In truth, they aren't so different. All the nose-men and eye-women of the city... you couldn't be late on your rent without half the world knowing about it, but break a child's arm, and, well, accidents happened. Some of the ways of the city are still the old ways, the very old ways, from when children were legally the property of their parents. Laws can change without attitudes or beliefs changing with them.

I should have talked to the great-aunt, I thought. Or the sister. But the parents probably wouldn't have let me. Closing ranks. It's a very old story.

Two blocks north, I tasted something in my chin. "This way," I said to Cott, and he let me lead him across the street and down a narrow alley, the taste growing stronger with every step, to where the boy was sitting, his back against a rusty chain-link fence, his butt on his school bag, his head in his hands. What do you know, I thought. I didn't have to use any of the old training, the techniques the finders of the municipal authorities undoubtedly were using. I found him with my chin. That wasn't something I was going to tell Cott.

"Do you see him?" I asked.

"I see a shadow." Cott was excited, happy. He squeezed my arm.

"Ellem," I said, and the boy shot to his feet, trembling, no talent or skill or charm-tasting needed to see his fear.

"I'm not going to hurt you," I said. Naturally he did not believe this. I saw no physical injury on him. His pain came from a different source. "I just want to know why you're hiding."

"We want to help you," Cott said.

"Cott, please."

"Your parents are very worried about you."

I saw it, then, in the boy's face, in his eyes. I tasted it, in my chin. I tasted it in my heart.

"But how can you take care of yourself," I said softly. "You're only eleven."

"I'll be twelve soon," Ellem said. He was terrified, and he was right to be terrified, for how could he know what sort of people Cott and I were, but he didn't crumble. He straightened. He looked directly at me. "You're a finder."

"Retired. Your charms won't last forever. What will you do then?"

"Get out of the city."

"How will you live? How will you eat?"

"I don't care."

Cott said, "What's going on?"

"He's trying to save his life," I said. "Can you see him yet?"

"No. The shadow is... a little more solid."

"Ellem, this man here, this man with me, is not a bad man. He has a temper, and he's stubborn, and impatient, but he's not a bad man. Will you let him touch you, just on the hand? One touch, on the hand. That's all. And then we'll leave you alone."

He was trapped. The only thing he could do was run, and there were two people standing between him and the entrance to the alley. Old people, yes, but one who was starting to look angry, and another who could find him despite his creation of a hiding spell. He lifted his right hand and stood stoically, as if braced for a blow.

I took Cott to him, and placed Cott's fingers on the back of the boy's hand. Then I lifted Cott's fingers away, and walked us back a few feet. The boy had stopped trembling, but his eyes were drops of despair.

"All right," I said to Cott. "You understand, now. Don't tell me you're so old you've lost your own skills."

Cott dropped my arm. His shoulders slumped, and he shook his head, and he didn't say anything.

"So now you're going to leave me alone," Ellem muttered. "Right? That's what you said."

"He can't hide forever," Cott said, to me, but not looking at me. "You were right about that."

I'd been right about more than that, but I didn't say it. I let him think. I let him be.

"Things like that shouldn't happen. Things like that should never happen."

"No, they shouldn't."

"The municipal authorities…"

Ellem's eyes widened.

"Cott. Let's go home."

"But he can't survive on his own. How can he survive on his own?"

"You think the municipal authorities will help him? A foster home, that's the best they'd be able to come up with." And, given the policy of family reunification, six months later he'd be back with his parents. Children belonged with their parents, after all.

"No!" Ellem shouted. "No! I'll turn myself to stone first."

He might have been able to do it, too, if he had enough charms left, with enough power in them, and enough talent. He certainly had enough desperation.

"You said he was trying to save his life. Now he's threatening that?"

"You can hear him."

"Yes. I can see him, too."

I had hoped for that.

Ellem stared at both of us, eyes wide, shaking again, fury mixed with his fear.

"Sometimes people have a good reason to hide," I said.

"He can't hide here, in an alley."

"You said you were going to leave me alone! So leave me alone!"

Cott looked at me, finally. "He could hide with us."

"Think that through," I said. "Take a minute, and think that through all the way."

"We have room. We have books and screens. He could study. And we could keep him safe. The finders haven't hooked a single thread. And if they come sniffing around, we can deflect them. I could. I know I could. I haven't lost my skills. You just saw that I haven't."

"He's eleven." I glanced at Ellem. "Almost twelve. That's six years, at least, of hiding him. And you have no idea whether this kid—" I couldn't say it. Would turn out to be the same sort of monster his father was.

"Are you the person I think you are," Cott said, "or have I been living with a stranger for fifty years?"

He didn't say those words with anger. That was unusual for him. It gave me a twinge.

"Who are you people?" Ellem said. "I mean, I know where you live. Down the street from me. But who are you? And how come you're changing, when you're so old?"

"Does that bother you, that I'm changing?"

"No," he said, after a moment. "It's just weird."

"Hiding in a house for six years might be better than hiding in an alley, even if we make you do lessons."

"You said this man wasn't a bad man. How about you?"

"You're going to have to decide that. About both of us. And if you do come to that conclusion, we won't make you stay. You'd be free to leave whenever you wanted. I promise."

"Like you promised to leave me alone." His voice was bitter. I knew that bitterness. It was rooted deeply in him, the same as it was rooted in me. He would not be able to give it up easily. He likely would not be able to give it up at all.

Cott was gazing at him now, gazing at the boy with longing. I understood that expression. This was what he had wanted all his life, and put away the hope of ever having.

What I said next was not for Ellem, but for Cott. I did not know Ellem, except in the way that members of the same, unchosen, tribe know each other, recognize each other. The boy would bring problems, a thousand problems. The boy would bring heartache. But Cott had carried a heartache for fifty years.

"Come with us," I said. "For a day. One day. And if tomorrow you want to leave, we will take you to the bus station, we will buy you a ticket, we will shield you from the eye-women and the nose-men, and the plainclothes Cleaners. A boy as brave as you can risk one day with two old people, can't you?"

"I have a knife," he said.

"That's good. I'd have a knife, too, if I were you."

"What's your favorite subject in school?" Cott asked.

The boy waited a few seconds before answering. "Math."

Please, I thought, don't ask him what he wants to be when he grows up.

"What about your sister," I asked. "Is she all right?"

"They never touched her. It was only me."

That happened, sometimes.

"If you stay close, you can keep an eye on her. Make sure she stays safe."

Something changed in Ellem's face, then. He looked down at his school bag. After a few moments, he picked it up.

We took him home. Cott kept trying to talk to him, which made people look at us, as nobody could see Ellem, since the hiding spell was still working strongly. Old people can stop being invisible in more ways than one. I didn't say anything to Cott. I let him be. And I let Ellem listen, not interrupting, even though I was afraid that Cott's enthusiasm would make the boy suspicious. He had every right to be suspicious, of course, to be suspicious of everyone in the world. But I hoped that through the chatter and the longing Ellem would catch a hint or two of Cott's goodness, or at least his good intentions.

The feathers sprouting from my scalp itched.

We put him in the guest room, which hadn't had a guest in it for years, and left him alone to calm down, to think things through himself, to struggle with fear and hope. Cott immediately started cooking. I let him be.

I had never wanted children, because I feared I would hurt them.

And when I was younger, I would have.

But things change. I looked into myself, and knew that however angry I became, and I could get angry just as easily as Cott did, though I never showed it, I would not hit Ellem. And I certainly would not do what his father had done and his mother had allowed his father to do. There are many ways to kill a child. It doesn't have to be with a knife, or a fist, or hands gripping a throat. I had only gotten the fists, and that had been enough to murder part of me, because the fists never stopped coming. Even now, the fists were there. But I did not have to raise my own. I might want to, I would always want to, but I would not do it. I could trust myself, and that was a remarkable thing to realize.

And Cott's anger, Cott's eagerness? His anger would be directed at Ellem's family first, the municipal authorities after that. I would have to keep him in check, using reason, using logic. We could not draw any attention to ourselves or to this house, if we were really going to do this thing. Cott's eagerness, the boy would have to deal with.

I went to my screen, and checked the local news. There was nothing new, nothing alarming.

Six years. We might both be dead by the time Ellem was legally safe from his family, and the municipal authorities. Of course, he might run off tomorrow, or next week. Or call on us to honor our promise to take him to the bus station.

Cott came into the room. There was noodle sauce on his shirt.

"I love you," he said.

"Are you all right?"

"I will be. You will be. We can do this."

"Don't even think about revenge. Promise me."

"I promise."

He would think about it, of course. He would turn it over and over in his mind, and not be able to sleep, and punch a wall, or take a swing at some young fool who ignored him in a shop. He wouldn't be able to help himself.

"To keep Ellem safe, we have to stay invisible."

"I understand that." He paused. "Thank you."

I wished he hadn't said that. It made me feel small.

"I told you that sometimes people have a good reason to hide." I kept looking at the screen, so as not to see his face.

"Yes," he said, and I heard him walk toward me, and stop just behind my chair. He leaned over, and picked up my hands. "And sometimes they don't." Then he bent further, and kissed my silver palms.

In Comes I

IT IS A WEEKDAY, AND SOON IT'LL BE TWELVE-THIRTY, SO I
have good reason to hope that if I walk down to the little
park on Bertolt Street now, she will be sitting there on the
bench underneath the poplar trees, sipping juice slowly
through a straw and smoothing back her hair as she turns
the pages of her magazine.

Gav, who lives on my left forearm, snickers at me.
*She'll never give you a second glance. Why would she? You're
useless and fat and ugly.* Gav, it appears, is in a mood today.
Then again, Gav usually is. It's difficult to blame him; his
life is a terribly circumscribed one, and it is certainly not
one he ever chose. The bitterness is understandable. I try
not to become impatient with him.

In any case, it doesn't matter if she looks at me or not.
It's enough, right now, for me to be able to look at her. For
a very long time, I've had to search hard, every day, for
something different to distract me from death. Perhaps it is
a result of age, but my attention span has been dwindling;
very little holds my interest for more than a few hours. Every
day I needed something new, something new, something
new, something different. It was tedious. It is tedious. To
fall into a routine like that can only lead to depression.
But ever since I glimpsed her in the park, last week, I have
not had to ferret out new distractions. This has been very
pleasant, despite Gav's negativity.

Look at you, you think you're in love. And he laughs, in
an exceedingly ugly manner.

I understand that Gav lashes out at me as a way of
dealing with his own pain. Pain shared is pain doubled,
after all. I brush my hair, I check my teeth, I stare into my
own eyes in the mirror, and suppress all outward sign of

injury. If I let him see that he's hurt me, even briefly, that even a whisker of his verbal cat o'nine tails has landed, the encouragement will drive him to greater efforts. On my birthday, last year, I broke down for a moment, and cried. Gav rejoiced for days. He was insufferable.

Of course I am not in love. There is no such thing as love.

She must work in one of the office buildings that line the north side of the park. She doesn't dress like a salesclerk, and she is too old to be a college student. Though I am no marvelous judge of ages, she appears to be in her thirties— late thirties, even. Her hair is long, reaching down to the middle of her back, and there is gray in it. Sometimes the wind blows a great wing of hair across her face while she is trying to read, and she pushes it off, laughing. Her hands are small. There is a red scar just above the last knuckle of her right hand. She doesn't wear nail polish.

I tie my shoelaces. I take my jacket off the closet doorknob. Gav quivers angrily, but he has closed his eyes, pursed his small mouth into a tight white line. This is what he does when he pretends to have resigned himself to something. It is a feint, a ploy. I am not fooled; I remain, as always, on my guard.

I feel so sorry for him. Though sentimentality is a weakness, though honesty also is a weakness, though I, too, did not choose this, before I open the door, before I put on my jacket, I stroke Gav's small, marble-round skull. He allows it. This time. Often, he tries to bite me. Occasionally, he succeeds. His tiny black teeth are as sharp as needles and always draw blood, but the wounds do not scar. "One day you will be free," I say, softly.

Gav growls, but does not open his eyes.

Outside, it is a beautiful day, a lovely warm afternoon. Afternoon, yes, but just barely. I have enough time to reach the little park on Bertolt Street. She arrives, has arrived, every weekday just after twelve-thirty, and sits and eats a muffin or a roll, and sips juice, and reads a magazine, until a few minutes to one. I think she must be a temp; temps get half-hour lunch breaks. She dresses in skirts and heels, so she must be working in an office. Something about her face makes me smile inside, and allows me not to think about death.

Under the sleeve of my jacket, Gav clenches his muscles. He is pretending to be asleep, but he is a very bad actor. He is plotting something; he plans to hurt me. I believe Gav would die, if he could. He has lost hope.

I didn't lie to him, when I said he'd be free one day, some day. I believe this is possible. I believe in the future. I still have hope.

The sun is warm and yellow, its rays beaming down friendly light. The air is mild. People walk to lunch in t-shirts and sandals; cars rumble past with their windows open. These are the golden days of spring.

Strolling, not too fast, not too anxiously, I decide I will… I will. I will introduce myself to her today.

Kids in blue pants and white shirts come pouring out of the charter school on Hyacinth. Tiny little kids; I believe the charter school only goes up to the first grade. I'm surprised the school lets them out for lunch. Ah, but probably the building doesn't have a cafeteria. It used to be a hardware store. The kids are happy, though, yelling and hopping up and down and swarming the guy with the hot dog cart who's parked himself at the corner. In the distance, I hear the music of an ice cream truck.

Introduce myself sounds so formal. Like a tongue-tied idiot in a suit at his first dance, sweating, spilling his drink. No, no, no. I try to picture it better—sitting down on the bench across from her, waiting until she glances up from the magazine (she always has a magazine)—smiling, nodding. Waiting until the next time she glances up, then saying Hi.

Pigeons dodge my feet. A squirrel makes a mad dash across my path, and I burst out laughing. Spring, spring, spring! This is not a day for anything, for anyone, to die.

You'd be better off doing crossword puzzles, Gav says. *What I wouldn't give to be able to do a crossword puzzle.*

To save some time, because I have dawdled, I take the shortcut across the triangle below Blue Street. The people who live down here have a lot of community pride. I see window boxes on many of the buildings, yellow flowers, red flowers, kitchen herbs growing healthy and green.

By the way, have I ever told you how much I despise your taste in clothes?

"All the time," I answer.

There is an empty parking lot next to a cluster of abandoned buildings. The buildings used to house a laundry, a liquor store, and a sandwich shop. The signs for the businesses are still there, but the windows are covered with metal shutters and the doors are boarded up. The parking lot is empty of cars, but not of people. There are a lot of people in the parking lot, standing in a circle, looking down at something, and I know right away this is a very bad thing.

Gav laughs to himself, and briefly, I hate him with a hot, fierce, painful hatred. One day I may very well lose my patience, lose my sympathy, throw away my compassion for his situation. I dream sometimes that I am holding Gav over the flames of my stove's front burner, grinning as he melts away. I wake up from these dreams sweating. Naturally, in real life, Gav wouldn't melt if I did that. He's not made of snow. He's solid, he is flesh, he's alive. Of course, I would never do it. It's silly to feel guilty about things that happen in your dreams.

I just wish that Gav would remember more often that while I can live without him, he can't live without me.

I try to duck away into an alley, but there are no alleys;

I'm in the middle of the block and the people in the parking lot across the triangle have spotted me. A tall man shouts, a short fat woman starts waving her arms. I turn my back on them, on the crowd that was looking at something terrible inside the parking lot and now is looking at me, but Gav turns me around again. He's giggling. He's enjoying himself, now. He knows I'm in a hurry, he knows she gets only half an hour for lunch. The people in the parking lot are being rather restrained, for a below-Blue-Street throng; they are not screaming, yet. The people who live below Blue Street are, in general, a demonstrative bunch. Emotional. Not inclined to be shy. Right now, a few of them are calling out, but more of them are waving me over, and most of them are simply waiting.

They will all start yelling if I walk away. I know; it's happened before. If I walk away, they will chase me down. I don't understand it; it isn't rational of them to do that. They can't force me to do anything. They can't hurt me, either. Or not very much. If they hurt me too much, Gav will lash out, lay them all on the ground, twitching and dripping pink froth from their mouths. Gav tends to remember that he can't live without me when I am attacked.

I turn around again and start to walk away.

Gav turns me back once more. The people in the parking lot are calling more loudly.

"I hate you," I tell him.

Not as much as I hate you.

Please come, please help. Please come, please help. They are shouting now, yelling. Death is there, of course. Something is dead. Perhaps many somethings.

I try to look at my watch, but Gav won't let me.

I am walking across the street, walking along the rusted chain-link fence outlining the lot, I am walking into the lot, and the people are parting before me, some of them, and others are reaching out to touch me, pat my shoulders, pat my face, pat my hair. I hate this. I hate this more than anything in the world.

The sun is very hot on the back of my neck. I want to close my eyes.

My voice is creaky, rusty. I don't know why, because I've been talking to Gav all day. To myself, I sound like an ancient door opening. "What is dead?"

The circle of lookers widens to let me in, to let me see.

"Don't touch me," I say, and they stop. Mostly. A couple of the older women keep patting me, lightly, grandma caresses.

Oh dear. Oh dear oh dear oh dear.

There are many dead.

"What is this?" I say. "What has happened? What has caused this?" But they don't know. They never know.

I suppose it doesn't matter; dead is dead, after all, and how the dead got dead perhaps is not so important. I would like to know, though, just out of curiosity. Gav doesn't care; he's jumping around under my sleeve, chortling with joy. I hate him; I hate him so bitterly the taste of it floods my mouth. But I understand, as well. He is bored, most of the time, disgusted with his inert, confined existence. If I didn't understand Gav's pain so well, I might nerve myself to take a knife, a razor, a sharp piece of glass, and…

Of course I would never do that. I am committed to finding a way to free us from each other. Free us of each other. There is a way. I am completely sure of that. We came together, and so we must be able to come apart.

I look at the dead. The throng in the parking lot murmur. They have stopped stroking me now, even the grandmas. I don't want to see this. I don't want to do this. Gav does; he's as thrilled as a child in an amusement park. He's yipping and chattering so loudly I'm sure everyone can hear.

It's hard to tell what the dead are. If they are human or not. This is not disturbing to me; I always have this difficulty. What is disturbing is simply that they are dead.

These dead are quite small. They might be children; they might be dogs, or perhaps very large cats. They might be adults who have been burned down to bone. I don't know. There are a dozen… no, perhaps two dozen of them, curled up and dark, on the broken pavement of the parking lot. They are motionless, of course. If these small dead have a smell, I cannot detect it; I haven't been able to smell a thing since Gav first began to live on me. Some of the corpses seem stuck to the ground, like half-melted candy bars. I'm beginning to think this might be the result of a fire, after all.

I'll never know for sure. Gav doesn't care. He's got only one thing on his mind.

Oh, he is happy. Happy, happy, happy. Deliriously so. I strip off my jacket and let it drop. I know it will disappear, will be torn to inch-long shreds by the crowd, the fragments passed around, bartered, kept, cherished. Better the jacket than me. I can buy another jacket. The thrift stores are full of them.

I kneel among the small dead. Gav rears up as far as he can stretch, opens his little gleaming eyes wider, opens his little wet mouth wider, opens his little clawed fingers the widest. I manage to snatch a glance at my watch.

Broken bits of the pavement dig into my knees, hurting me, but the biggest pain is in my heart. It is a quarter to one. Before I am done here, she'll be gone from the bench under the tree in the park on Bertolt Street, disappeared into one of the office buildings, which one I don't even know. I won't get to see her today. I won't get to look at her. I won't get to smile, and say hi, and maybe introduce myself. This loss hurts so much tears bite my eyes.

I might not ever see her again. Today may have been my last chance. People move, change jobs, alter their routines. Tomorrow she might eat lunch somewhere else.

Ecstatically, Gav goes to work. He really throws himself into it. His whole body quivers with joy. Around me, the crowd murmurs. Someone starts to clap his hands. Soon they will be singing. I know. They always do.

As the small dead begin to stir, to blink, to gulp in air and cry out, to rise and look around with wonder, to shake themselves and live again, I kneel on the hard sharp ground and cry silently, because today I would have spoken to her, I would have smiled at her and she would have smiled at me, I would have learned her name and she would have asked me for mine. Today was no day for anyone, for anything, to die.

REDEMPTION

FOUR MONTHS DELIVERING PIZZAS FOR LA BOCCA GRANDE, Austin knew all the stories. The fat lady who came to the door naked. The latchkey kid who handed over two dollars and twelve cents on an order that came to eleven-fifty. The guy who loosed his pitbull at you so you'd drop the box and run. The old woman who forgot she'd placed an order and wouldn't let you in, then called the shop five minutes later complaining her pizza hadn't arrived. The guy whose delivery you did not want to take, even though he was a good tipper, since when he opened up the door the smell from his big old unwashed self would choke a swamp gator.

That was the easy stuff, the experiences he could laugh about, turn into a funny story over a beer with his roommate Jerry or recount in a phone call to Yolanda, his almost-ex girlfriend. *Let me tell you about the idiot who came in today, wanted us to dry clean his fucking beach towel, she'd say. Oh yeah? Let me tell you about the college boy who puked on my goddamn new BK's, then asked me if I had change for a fifty, he'd say.*

Amusing anecdotes.

Then there were the once-upon-a-time stories. The celebrity who handed over a hundred-dollar tip, the hot girls who handed over sex, the eccentric recluse who handed over the secret of immortality. The seven little dudes who paid in gold, the guy with donkey ears, the old witch and her talking rats. Austin didn't believe a word of these stories, but they were sort of fun to listen to if you were drunk enough.

There were other things that weren't fun at all, that none of the delivery guys or the oven guys or the phone guys talked about much after they happened. One time, some kids phoned in a forty dollar order, the address almost out of their delivery zone, way on the north end of Lake Street. But for forty bucks you go, and the guy who went got the crap beat out of him and his money and car taken. One time, there was a delivery to the Heights, upscale, yeah, where the doctors and stock brokers lived. Man came to the door with a gun and shot the delivery guy in the face. Didn't kill him. Blew his face off, but didn't kill him. One time, this normal order came in, repeat customer, large pie with mushrooms and a side of garlic breadsticks. Man invited the delivery guy in, said *hold on a minute, I left my wallet on the TV,* hit the guy, tied him up, worked him over with a knife and other shit, killed him. Nobody told those stories, but they always popped into the back of Austin's mind whenever an order came in that seemed… off.

We Deliver Late, La Bocca Grande proudly proclaimed on its red white and green sign and its red white and green flyers, and Austin's shift was six to twelve. It had been a slow night, just a couple of short runs. He'd burned more in gas and aggravation than he'd made in tips, so he perked up when the phone shrilled and the telephone guy started scratching on his pad. "Mine," Austin said, though Leodan, the other delivery guy on Wednesdays, was also hanging out with his thumb up his ass, drinking Cokes and bugging Maricela the counter girl. Leo had had more runs tonight than him, so Austin felt cool calling this one.

Stefano, the phone guy, was taking too long getting the info, though. Usually it was, "Yeah, yeah, yeah," scratch scratch scratch with his goddamn soft lead pencil, "twenty minutes." Austin stood up, came around the partition between the back tables and the kitchen area. A little tickle of unease began to stir in the space between his shoulder blades.

"Yes, sir. Twenty minutes." Stefano hung up the wall phone. His eyes were narrow, unhappy.

"What?"

"Carlton Street. Three pies," he said, ripping the top sheet off the order pad.

"Yeah, but what?"

"Guy was calling from a pay phone."

Which meant Stefano hadn't gotten a home call-back number in case they needed to check the order, check the address.

"Legit?"

"I think so. Guy said he was on his way home. Called on the way to make sure he didn't miss last delivery."

"His address in the system?" The system being the boss's kid's castoff Mac, humming on the counter under the wall phone.

Stefano shook his head. "First time customer."

"Shit," Austin said.

"You want the run or not?" Stefano held out the order slip. "Cause Leo looks free."

"Shit." He snatched the slip. "I'll take it."

☙

Carlton Street was low-rent residential, two-story eight-unit buildings mixed with three-story three-family houses, all of which, from the mailboxes outside, looked to house at least six families. No high rises, no private homes. Austin, cruising slowly, searching for the address, thought the area looked nicer than his neighborhood. The garbage cans were all chained up, and they all had lids; the three-family houses had two-car ground-level garages. Of course, if you hauled up the sliding door on any of those garages, what you'd find behind it would most likely be a makeshift dorm and a lot of tired men in their underwear, but still the garages and the tarred driveways gave the neighborhood an air of class. Kinda like the suburbs.

437 Carlton, apartment 1D. The building was low, squat, a twin of the one directly across the street from it. A long time ago, someone had decided to put aluminum siding on both of them. Bad idea. The lighting was pretty good, though, a streetlight in the middle of the block, and house lights on the twin. No house lights on 437, but Austin could read the numbers okay. He hated it when he had to get out of the car and guess in the dark.

Okay, 1D would be in the back. Austin unzipped the red keep-hot case, hauled out the three pizza boxes. The aroma of hot cheese mixed with warm oil mixed with baked cardboard whooshed up into his face. He'd stopped finding this smell appetizing about two weeks into this gig. Now pizza was just something he ate every day, because he and Leo got the leftovers from the slice trays free at the end of the night. Taking the boxes out of the keep-hot case was a no-no, the boss wanted them to haul the carry-case to the client's door, unzip it there, but that took time, and Austin wanted to be in and out fast. Boss would never know, anyway. Got the bill slip. $26.97. Son of a bitch had better give him more than a three-cent tip.

Damn. *Hot*. Austin held the boxes by the sides, but the heat still scorched his fingers.

437 had a foyer. He shoved the door with his shoulder, and it swung open—good, no springlock. 437 had a row of mailboxes with doorbells set into them. Yeah, good. 1D. Austin ducked his head, pressed the button with his chin, held it down hard until he heard the ding-ding echoing from inside the building.

The foyer's second door, the one opening on the first floor hall, was a flimsy thing, old wood and old glass windows. A white curtain hung over the windows on the inside of the door. Austin hoped the guy would come out and open up, not just buzz him in.

He hit the bell again. *Come on, man, I'm burning my fingers off here.*

Fuck it. Austin set the boxes on the floor of the foyer. Boss would have a shitfit if he saw that, but fuck it. Austin flapped his fingers in the air, then blew on them. That helped a little. Then he thought, three pies for one guy, and went, "Fuck!" out loud. This *was* a gag, a street kid phoning in a late order to nowhere, so the pies would get tossed in the back dumpster when Austin got back to the shop after closing time, easy pickings for the hungry. Motherfucking waste of time, motherfucking waste of his life…

Just for the hell of it, he tried the knob of the inner door. It turned; the door opened.

Great security they had in this place.

The hall floor was dingy brown linoleum, the walls almost the same shade of brown, though probably they'd started out as tan or something. There was one light above the inner door, a bare bulb, maybe forty watts. Made the place look like an abandoned tunnel. Stairs to his left, but he didn't have to worry about stairs. Closed doors to the left and right, one with a very tired-looking Christmas wreath on it. 1A, 1B. He didn't have to worry about them, either. As he'd figured, 1D was at the ass end of the corridor.

Shit.

Austin picked up the three pizza boxes. Less hot, but still *hot*, goddamn it. He walked to the ass end of the shit-brown corridor, set the boxes down on the dusty floor, and knocked sharply on the door of 1D. "Hello! Pizza!"

A couple of seconds later, a voice called from inside the apartment. "Come in."

Then another, "Come in!"

And another: "Come IN!"

Female voices. Soprano, mezzo, alto. Loud, bold, though sort of strained. Sort of eager. Come in? What was up with this place, nobody locked any freaking doors here?

And what happened to the guy? Stefano said it was a guy who'd phoned in the order.

Fuck me, Austin thought. "Pizza!" he shouted again, just to make double-damn-sure, and opened the apartment door.

It was dark inside. Pizza boxes back in his hands, Austin stood on the threshold, peering into shadow. Goddamn it to hell, this was going to be one of those days, wasn't it? The apartment smelled of spider webs and dust, mouse droppings and very old pillows. Crack whores, he thought. That explained why all the doors were unlocked. Easy access. Cheap-ass crack whores, or broke-ass crack whores, who couldn't get it together to keep the electricity on. Wonderful. And what were the odds these three had thirty bucks on them?

Austin made out some darker shadows in the gloom, more solid, closer to the ground. They're sitting on the floor, he thought. Great. They got no furniture, either. Probably just a couple of mattresses, for business purposes. I'm gonna fucking kill Stefano when I get back to the shop.

"Hello," he called into the darkness, as politely as he was able, given that he was thoroughly pissed off and expected to be stiffed. "Can I get a little help here?"

A sigh came from the darkness, or perhaps three sighs, exhaled simultaneously. The crack whore with the lowest voice said, "I'm afraid we are unable to help you, young man." She sounded sad about that.

Shit. A crack whore with a vocabulary. Maybe once upon a time she'd been an English major. "I got three pizzas here," Austin said.

"Thank you."

"Thank you."

"Thank you."

"It comes to $26.97."

"Come in," the women told him, three times.

Austin lost his cool. It was pretty clear he wasn't going to get his $26.97, and it was also pretty clear that he was going to leave the damn pizzas anyway and take the hit out of his already-tiny paycheck, because at this point it wasn't worth the aggravation of hauling them back to the shop and tossing them into the dumpster. He'd been played for a sucker, and he was going along with it, so the least these bitches could do was stop jerking him around. "Fuck! I can't see for shit, *ladies*. You think I'm gonna break my neck for you sluts? You want your fucking pizzas, you fucking haul your lazy stoned asses over here and get them."

The woman with the mellow, mid-range voice said, "Young man, we regret that we are unable to come to the door. But if you will be patient a moment, I believe some illumination can be provided."

Fucking hell. Two English majors. Austin was getting completely, thoroughly teed off. They were playing him up and down and sideways. He didn't have time for this shit. He considered throwing the pizzas on the floor and stomping out.

There was a soft click, and a small burst of light popped up in the back of the darkness. The back of the apartment. A dim bulb in a shaded lamp, the rosy light so gentle it did not startle his eyes. "Come in," each of the three voices commanded him again, and Austin sighed through his teeth and stepped into the skanky-smelling apartment, the pizza boxes in his hands beginning to sag now as the oil soaked through the cardboard. "Okay, okay, here's your goddamn order, and so where's my twenty—" *six ninety seven* died in his mouth.

The three women were not sitting on the floor. There was no mattress, there was no furniture of any kind in the room. The lamp was a lamp, though, an old brass thing with a thick paper shade, and it was plugged into a wall socket and everything. The lamp was normal. Austin held onto that fact fiercely: the lamp is normal, at least; well, at least, you know, the lamp is normal.

The three women were naked, the upper parts of their bodies, anyway, which was all of them that he could see. The three women were in a row, each separated from the next by an arm's length, and each one was buried to the waist in the floor.

There had been no accident. They had not fallen, one after the other, through rotten floorboards. The floor was solid. Some kind of weird bondage game, Austin thought wildly, but that wasn't it, either. No one had sawed holes in the floor for fun. No one had sawed holes, period. The women were fixed in the floor, as firmly and organically as if their upper bodies had grown out of it, like trees.

Not one of them looked happy about it. The three women gazed at him with melancholy expressions. In his first moment of terror, Austin had thought the three women had the same face, that they were triplets, or clones of each other, but now he saw that they were very different. He had no idea which voice belonged to whom, but one of the women was very thin, scrawny, really, with a narrow, almost jawless face and long, feathery hair that looked blond in the soft lamplight. The middle woman had big hooters, which sagged less than the sets on the other two, and which Austin had a little trouble taking his eyes off of. She had dark, dark nipples. Her face was round and full-cheeked, and her hair had been shaved off pretty recently; short black fuzz, little more than stubble, covered her skull. The last woman was older than the other two. Austin had no desire to look at her breasts, which lay flat on her chest like wrinkly, stretched out pancakes. This woman had iron gray hair in a braid down her back, and a not-so-faint white mustache. They were very, very different, but Austin saw why at first glance they had seemed alike. Each woman wore the same expression, a look of gentle, restrained anticipation. Not hopeful, nothing as positive as that, but sweet, sad, expectant.

They were waiting.

They looked like they had been waiting a long, long time, and had gotten way, way expert in all the different permutations and combinations of the process, had become grandmasters of the methodology.

The three women in the floor smiled at Austin. The skinny one had rotten teeth. The big-boobed one didn't show hers; she smiled with her mouth closed. The old one smiled with her mouth open, but didn't have any teeth to show.

"Where the fuck are your legs?" Austin said.

The old woman spoke. She had a sugar-sweet, soprano voice. "Perhaps one day they shall be redeemed."

Big-breasts, who turned out to be the mezzo, said sadly and sweetly, "We are under a curse, through none of our own doing. We suffer thus, as you see, bound in this place, suspended between life and death."

The skinny one, the alto, asked, "Is there any pepperoni on those pizzas?"

"Nah," Austin said. "Three plain." Then he said, "No shit. A curse?"

"We are hungry," the oldest one said, her voice high, and gentle, and unhappy.

"Yeah," Austin said, and then something in his brain clicked and he said, "Yeah, I mean, right! Okay." He knelt on the dusty floor and set the pizza boxes down. *One time I went on this run, and I found three naked ladies in an empty room. Oh man, was this going to be a story.* Austin tore open the lid of the top box, lifted it off the stack, then carried it to the oldest woman. How she was going to eat it without any teeth, he had no idea. *Once upon a time, I delivered to three women under a curse, suspended between life and death.* He opened the second box, set it down in front of the skinny one, who nodded and smiled at him gratefully. *Hey, Jerry, what's up, Yolanda, guess what happened to me today.* Austin set the third box before the big-breasted one. It wasn't his fault he was at eye-level with them. He wouldn't tell Yolanda that part. The first two were already scarfing down slices, the old one sucking the topping off the crust and gumming it like mad, the skinny one chewing real fast, though wincingly, with her decayed teeth. Big-boobs looked at him measuringly before she reached for the food. Austin found himself backing up. Backing up pretty swiftly. Backing up almost to the door. A look of gentle melancholy was not the only type of expression this lady was capable of. His heart was pounding hard.

The three women bolted down their pizzas like they hadn't eaten for days. For all he knew, they hadn't. Be careful, he wanted to say, you're gonna get sick, you're gonna try to gulp too big a chunk and choke. Austin didn't fancy trying the Heimlich maneuver on a torso which had everything below the belly-button trapped inside a floor. The pizza was going to make them thirsty, too, and they had nothing to drink, no soda, no water even.

A curse, he thought. Fucking hell.

He wondered what would happen when the food worked its way, as food did, through their systems. They ate, so it was only logical that eventually they would have to... Austin flinched away from the image that popped into his mind.

"Are you gonna be okay?" he asked. The women glanced up at him, eyes wide and moist, but they were too busy chewing and swallowing to answer. Austin figured it was a fucking stupid question anyway. Sunk into the floor in a ratty old building on Carlton Street. Couldn't even scratch their asses if they itched. If they even had asses any more. Sure they were going to be okay.

This was wrong. This was so wrong. Sure, yeah, you got a beef with someone, you went and worked them over. Maybe you totally lost it and cut their throats and set the whole place on fire to cover it up, and never mind the kiddies living on the floor above. That kind of stuff he could understand, though it was wrong, too. This? This was evil of a deeper sort. This was torture, a torment that never stopped, never eased, for even a second. He could tell, just by their faces, that the three women had been here for a very long time.

The old one swallowed hard, and cleared her throat. "Thank you for the food," she said.

She was the one who'd said something about one day maybe getting their legs back, Austin thought. Something about getting redeemed. Like a pawn ticket.

"Thank you."

"Thank you."

"Is there," Austin said, and faltered. "I mean, what do... what would..." His thoughts slopped over each other; he wasn't sure what the fuck it was he wanted to say. Then, a second later, he was. "Can I help you?" Because it was very fucking clear that these three needed help, and he was just standing there, and what's a person supposed to do, anyway?

Austin could walk away after witnessing a car accident. He'd done it. Once he'd seen a guy he'd known slightly, met maybe twice, getting the living snot beat out of him by three drunken goons on the street outside the Donkey Bar at three a.m. He'd walked away from that, too, telling himself it was none of his business. This was none of his business, either, but the pain in the three women's eyes made the back of his throat burn.

The trapped women stopped eating. They looked at each other; the dim lamplight could not conceal the sudden eagerness, the raw hope and the new, sharper hunger in their expressions. The skinny one dropped her just-started slice and wiped shaking hands on her long, feathery hair. The other two stretched their arms as far as they could reach and each clasped the tips of the other's fingers. The oldest woman and the big-breasted one did not look at Austin. Their eyes were locked on each other. They were trembling. Austin's heart caught. *Shit*, he thought, *they're so scared, they want this so much...*

"Beware, beware," the skinny one said, but not to him. *They're scared to hope.*

"Can the curse be broken?" he asked.

"Yes," the old one said, in a whisper.

A qualm struck him. He knew, he absolutely fucking knew, that he was about to make a big mistake here. "Is it hard?"

"Yes," answered the big-breasted one, firmly. Now she turned her eyes to him. They were wet.

For some reason Austin's mouth had gone real dry. "Do you think I can do it?" he asked, in a small voice.

"You can, if you are steadfast," the skinny one said.

Austin wasn't quite sure what steadfast meant, but at least she didn't say *you can if you're as smart as a brain surgeon*, or *you can if you're as brave as a mugger on crank*, or *you can if you're as pure as a twelve-year-old virgin*, or something like that. "Okay," he said. "Tell me what the deal is. What do I have to do to get you ladies out of this situation?"

They told him. In fact, they explained it to him three times, partly, he thought, because each of the women wanted her own turn, and partly to make sure he understood all the details one hundred per cent. There were three parts to what he had to do to break the curse, which didn't surprise him; three seemed the standard number here. There was a task, a time period, and a condition.

The first time, Austin listened in disbelief, and almost burst out laughing. The second time, he listened very closely, with his full, complete attention, to be certain they weren't shitting him. After the third time, he couldn't help himself, and blurted out, "That's pretty fucking ridiculous. I mean, you gotta know that."

"That is our fate."

"We did not lay the curse on ourselves, and we did not decide on the manner of its undoing."

"We cannot change it."

Austin rubbed his eyes. Then he glanced at his watch. Holy shit. The shop had closed half an hour ago, and he hadn't checked in. The boss was gonna be pissed.

But then, the boss was going to be the least of his problems, if he actually went through with this.

"I don't suppose there's a reward, is there?" he asked. "You know, if I do it, like succeed? Gold, jewels, a flying carpet, something like that?"

No, the three women told him, one sadly, one resignedly, one angrily. Then they asked him if he would bind himself to make the attempt, one listlessly, one flatly, one boldly.

Austin sighed. He looked at the three women trapped in the dusty floor, their half-eaten pizzas growing cold in front of them. He sighed again. He never expected to say what he said next. He said, "Yes."

<hr />

Thank you.
　　Thank you.
　　　Thank you.

Their words echoed in Austin's head, the last words the three women spoke to him before he left the apartment on Carlton Street. He heard them as he paced the streets of the city, head down, scouring the sidewalks. He heard them when people laughed at him, when kids in knee-length white t-shirts tripped him and knocked him down and rubbed his face into the concrete for being a freak, when

Yolanda came running out of a café and made like she was going to grab his arm, but then just stopped dead, stared him in the face, and burst into tears. He heard them when the rain poured down and he huddled under a shoe store awning until the shoe store guy came out and chased him back into the storm, he heard them when the first snow fell and he just sat on a bus stop bench and cried, because he'd forgotten about snow, and how that would make the task so much harder it seemed all but fucking impossible. He heard them in his sleep.

A task, a time period, a condition.

He knew from the start that the condition would be hard. Or he thought he knew. *Man, that's gonna be a real bitch*, he had thought to himself, but he hadn't thought it through enough, worrying more about the time period and the task itself. The boss fired him inside a week, and with no job he couldn't make the rent, and inside a month he was on the street 24-7. He hadn't seen that coming. He'd thought he could manage by writing shit down, but it turned out people didn't want to be reading notes scribbled on his cheap-ass legal pad from the ninety-nine cent store. When he held the pad up to a customer with *That will be $11.99, sir. Thank you very much*, the customer just stared at him and then called the shop to complain; the boss yelled at him and Stefano called him a douche bag and Leo just twirled his finger by his ear and laughed, and Austin's ass was out of there. No job, no money, no home. Holding up a sign asking for spare change on the street didn't rake in the big bucks, either. He found more coins just by walking with his head down and his eyes on the pavement. Austin was hungry most of the time, though people threw so much food away that usually he got something to eat every day. Being tired all the time, bone-tired, sleepwalking, getting rousted from park benches, rousted from doorways, from alleys, from vacant lots, was way worse.

The condition: *not to bathe, nor shave, nor speak a word to any soul living or dead while endeavoring to accomplish the task he had been set.*

The time period: *a year and a day.* Austin had cringed at that. Sure, the way the three women in the floor said it, they made it sound all poetical and shit, but even caught up in the moment the way he'd been, he'd realized that the literal meaning of what he was hearing translated to *a fucking hell of a long time.* A whole fucking year, and if that wasn't enough, an extra damn day tacked on to it. It's cool, he'd told himself, I'll get the task done faster than that, I don't have to take three hundred and sixty-six days to do it in, I just gotta do it within that time, and that thought was comforting at first, in the very beginning. The very, very beginning, before he'd actually gotten started.

The task: *to collect three thousand used band-aids from the streets of the city, and return with them, inside of a year and a day, to the apartment in the building on Carlton Street, to lay one thousand used band-aids on the floor before each of the trapped women.*

You gotta be fucking shitting me, he'd said. Fucking band-aids?

They are a token, the three women told him. A symbol. It is the task that matters. The details are only symbols. But you must gather one thousand, no more, no less, for each of us.

And then we will rise, they told him. *We shall be redeemed. We will be free.* And when he agreed to take up the task, they thanked him with their sad, sweet, eager voices, and their thanks echoed inside Austin's head like music as he walked, and walked, and bent, and picked up a grubby, lost band-aid, and another, and another, day after day, week after week, month after month.

Jeez, people lost a lot of band-aids. Hell of a lot more than he would've figured. The park was good, the playground the best, though he had to scour it early in the day, before the children and their watchful parents arrived. Not that he blamed the parents; he saw his own reflection in store windows, and if he had been them he would have called the police on himself in a second. Cop cars patrolled the park regularly, too, and Austin had to be alert. Cops couldn't do anything to him for just walking down the street with his head down. The park was a different story.

Late spring was good, which was when he started, and summer was even better, kids with boo-boos on their knees losing their coverings all over the damn place, women with new sandals changing their band-aids on the courthouse steps, casually tossing the old, blood-spotted ones aside, guys playing more sports, banging up their shins, their elbows, their fingers, slapping on the band-aids clumsily, awkwardly, dropping the damn things all over the city. Spring and summer were good, and Austin crouched in the hidey-hole he'd found, under the rotten-through bleachers of the abandoned soft-ball field, counting his haul, sorting them into three plastic bags. He had decided to be fair, that he would not fill one bag and then start the next, but have three bags, and allocate his gatherings in equal numbers. More counting for him, but that was okay. He stored his collection there, under the bleachers, but didn't sleep there, didn't stay longer than necessary, because the field had been closed, the whole section of the park on the list for a brown-fields cleanup, ever since some alderman found out that the damn thing had been constructed on top of the site of an old factory, and there was shit like mercury and lead and crap like that in the soil. The field had been chained off, and even though the chain was rusted and the fence bent up in spots, even the high school kids looking for a private place to screw tended to avoid the soft-ball field.

Spring and summer. Okay. Sometimes he found criss-crossed band-aids, sometimes he found three of them together. Those seasons, the seeking was good.

Austin's beard grew, his hair, his fingernails. Bugs bit him, bugs laid eggs on him, bugs hatched and crawled over every inch of his skin. He stank. He itched. Around July, his teeth started to hurt like crazy, and the left side of his face swelled up like a muskmelon. He saw Jerry, his ex-roommate, outside a bar on Denby Street, and Jerry didn't recognize him. A rash started at the base of his spine and grew upwards, branching out to cover both shoulders. It itched worse than the bug bites, worse than the poison ivy he'd had once as a kid, and Austin took to rubbing his back against the pebble-dash walls of the big bank on Garnet Avenue, like an animal, like a pig he'd seen on TV, scratching itself against the side of its sty.

After the first few weeks, though, he didn't miss not speaking. He became comfortable with it. When Austin thought about it, that comfortableness scared him, so he tried not to think about it. Besides, it wouldn't be forever. None of this, not the pain or the dirt or the shame, not the hunger nor the exhaustion nor the silence, would last long. This wasn't his life. This was for merely one year and a day.

So the spring and summer passed, and Austin survived, enduring his suffering and battling through the discouragements, for even the most successful day, a day when he gathered twenty or thirty of the gummy, stained, germ-laden plastic strips from the streets of the city and the gravel of its playgrounds, brought its discouragement. Then fall arrived, sudden and chill, and both life and the mission became much more difficult. People wore more clothes, hiding their bandages under long sleeves, under socks, under jeans. Kids stayed indoors more, played on their computers instead of on swings. Summer jocks put away their basketballs and bike helmets. Women started to wear fuzzy, knee-high boots.

Austin began hanging around the community clinic on West Street, where weary-faced nurses drew blood for lab tests. Young guys, tough guys, would peel the band-aids off their arms as they came out of the clinic, wad them up, toss them away. That was cool; Austin waited in the parking lot of the store-front church across the street, pretending to read a salvaged newspaper, or drawing pictures in the little notebook he still carried with him. But the clinic was dangerous; every once in a while someone who worked there would approach him with the set, determined look that meant she was going to offer help, a shelter referral, the address of a drop-in center, the name of a soup kitchen, and he would have to flee.

When the first snow fell, early in November, Austin was bludgeoned by despair. Idiot, moron, dumbass; he'd forgotten that it would snow, that it always snowed in this city in wintertime. Even at the height of summer, there'd been days when he hadn't found a single discarded band-aid. He told himself, though, that as long as he could average ten a ten, a measly ten a day, he'd be set, he'd be through in plenty of time. Fucking shit-for-brains, forgetting about snow; all his calculations were off. Austin sat in the snow and cried. He'd slacked off, he hadn't hunted as hard as he could have, because he hadn't realized he'd lose the winter months.

He saw Yolanda for the second time on a subsequent day of snow, a day when Austin sat huddled in the scant windbreak of a bus stop shelter and contemplated giving this whole stupid thing the fuck *up* already. He'd contemplated a couple of other desperate actions, as well, over the past few days, like stealing a bunch of boxes of band-aids from various pharmacies, ripping them open, peeling each plasticized strip out of its paper wrapper, scattering them to the wild winds, and then assiduously picking them up again. He knew, though, that even discounting the danger of getting caught shoplifting, that it was a bad idea. If you're playing with magic and you try to cheat, you are one hundred per cent sure to get screwed.

Yolanda got off a bus, saw him hunched up on a corner of the bench, and went, "Oh fuck," in a voice like she'd almost stepped on something grotty. A knife went through Austin's heart. True, he and Yolanda had been more or less about to break up before he'd made the delivery run out to Carlton Street, but it still hurt to hear her use that tone. Austin buried his face in his arms. He didn't want to move, to stand up and push past her, because he'd lose the small respite of the bus shelter. Damn, the first time she saw him on the street, she'd felt sorry for him, and now she was all Oh fuck how repulsive and shit. How people fucking changed. He wished she'd just go away.

Yolanda went away.

She came back a few minutes later with a cup of coffee.

Austin took it, wrapped his hands around its heat gratefully, and sipped slowly and with appreciation, but Yolanda kept talking, talking, talking at him, and it was nice and all that she'd brought him coffee, he took back the nasty things he'd been thinking about her a few minutes ago, but she was getting on his nerves. Austin sipped, slowly, relishing the rush of caffeine, and kept his eyes closed.

Yolanda went away again. She returned with a pair of gloves and a wool hat she must have bought at the discount store one block up. She put them down on the bench next to him. "Fuck, Austin. I mean, fuck. Just look at yourself. You need help." Austin put on the hat, pulling it down low over his ears. It was blue. He'd always liked blue. The gloves were knock-offs, supposed to be that Thinsulate stuff but weren't, but what could you expect from a discount store. It was hard getting them on over his swollen knuckles and long, scraggly fingernails, but Austin managed it. Then it was hard picking up the coffee cup again, but he managed that, too.

Austin felt very grateful. He wanted to let Yolanda know that, so he took a risk, and looked up at her, met her eyes, and smiled.

Yolanda flinched like he'd hit her. "Oh, Austin," she said, in almost a whisper. "I mean, goddamn. Come on. Come on, I'll buy you dinner. Shit, I'll take you home and let you sleep on the couch, if you say something. *Talk* to me."

He had to get up and leave then, though he was sorry. Austin shook his head at her, tried to send thoughts: *later, I'll explain it all later, once upon a time I made a delivery out on Carlton Street*, but telepathy worked as well between them now as it ever did, which was not at all. Yolanda was pissed; Austin could feel her glaring at his back as he shuffled down the street. He'd make it up to her one day, he thought. When this was over.

For somehow, between the time Yolanda handed him the coffee and the time she came back with the hat and gloves, Austin had got his hope back. Okay, it was winter. Okay, he'd be lucky if he found one or two band-aids a day in the slush and rock-salt grit of the streets. But that was no excuse to give up. He'd do the best he could this season, he'd keep his eyes peeled and he'd walk the main streets doggedly, check out the clinic frequently. Schools. Kids still ran around in school courtyards. Kids still lost band-aids from their fingers and stuff, even in winter time, because they always forgot to put their gloves and mittens on. He'd have to be careful there, make those rounds after four, four-thirty, after the kids had gone home but while there was still some light left. Okay. And in the spring, he'd redouble his efforts, work until he frigging dropped if he had to. Determination swelled in his chest, warming him more than the coffee. He was going to do this, he was going to beat this thing, he was going to win. He'd quit everything else in his lousy life before, quit or been fired, quit or been dumped first, quit on his own damn self, but Austin wasn't going to bail on this. Not this, not this time.

Hope and determination kept him going through the long, tough winter, and into the late-arriving, slushy spring.

Austin gathered discarded band-aids, and survived the days and the nights, and fell asleep and woke to the music of the three trapped women's thanks echoing in his head, until one day in early April, when the kids were in shorts again and the women had all bought new sandals. He was smiling to himself under his mountain-man's beard, for he'd be gathering them up in handfuls now, only a few hundred left to go; the last time he'd been back to the bleachers he'd sat and counted and recounted and started grinning like a fool, because he'd seen the light at the end of the damn tunnel. He was really going to pull it off, until that day in April when Yolanda came to rescue him.

⌘

She came with a couple of guys, one of whom Austin later found out was her new boyfriend, and the other one some guy she knew from work. The guy from work had a car, which was how they sneaked up on him. Austin had been having a good day, almost a great day; he'd found seven band-aids already and it was only two in the afternoon. His heart was light. His spirit was firm. He was walking on Lake Street, with his head down. He spotted another one, bent, and grabbed it. He had it in his fingers. He was just straightening up when the two guys jumped out of the car and tackled him.

He hit the pavement hard, two guys on his back, and the band-aid flew out of his hand. Austin had been beaten up before, and his first reaction was to go limp, not fight, not give his attackers the least excuse to hit him more than they were already going to. He would have tried to curl up, cover his head, if he could have, but the guys were holding his arms, so Austin just shut his eyes and let himself go loose. Instead of punching the crap out of him or grinding his face into the sidewalk, the two guys hauled him to his feet. Opening his eyes in alarm and surprise, he saw Yolanda standing next to an idling car, and understood that something much worse than a bashing was going down here.

"We're going to help you," Yolanda said, her fists clenched, her voice shaking. She looked pale, which was scary-weird on someone with naturally olive skin. "You need help."

Austin began to fight, then. He twisted violently, breaking the grip of one of the guys holding him, and rammed his elbow into the second guy's belly. The first guy lunged at him, and Austin kicked him just above the knee, which made the guy stagger, but didn't put him down. First guy landed a punch to the side of Austin's head that made a small nova burst bright, then dark, behind his eyes. The second guy bear-hugged him and wrenched him off his feet. The first guy tried to grab Austin's legs, and Austin kicked up, wildly, forcing the guy holding him to jump back, but the kick didn't connect.

"We're going to help you," Yolanda screamed.

In a panic, Austin bucked and twisted; the first guy closed in again, and Austin whacked him on the chin with his forehead. "Motherfucker," the guy said, grimly, and then it got bad.

They slammed his head into the wall of a gone-out-of-business Brazilian barbecue restaurant; blood flooded Austin's mouth. They banged his head into the wall a couple more times. His arms felt heavy; his legs leaden. His thoughts were gummed up, like someone had opened up the top of his skull and poured in a pitcher of syrup. Yolanda didn't say a word to either of the men. She just watched.

They got him on the pavement again, face down, one of them kneeling on his back, pinning him down. The other one yanked Austin's arms out away from his sides. He lifted his head off the sidewalk, and the guy kneeling on his back shoved his face down again. Then the other guy stomped on Austin's right hand with the full force of his two hundred-some pounds. Pain blazed through him like red lightning, but he didn't scream, too shocked, the small, personal sound of his hand-bones snapping louder in his ear than the thud of the guy's steel-toed boot. Then the guy walked around to the other side, and Austin jerked liked a hooked fish, *my hands, I can't gather the band-aids with broken hands*, and without thought, raging with terror and despair, he opened his mouth and yelled, "No!" just as the man's boot came down on his left hand.

He realized. Instantly. Even before the word was out of his mouth.

Austin went still. He let the guys pick him up and dump him in the back seat of the car. He let Yolanda put her hand on his forehead and murmur nonsense to him. He let them drive him, after Yolanda spoke to her boyfriend sharply, to the emergency room, and at the emergency room he told the triage nurse his name, and his age, and that he wasn't allergic to anything. He didn't care how they looked at him, he didn't care what they did to him. Afterwards, cleaned up some, hands and wrists encased in bulky white casts, he let Yolanda take him home. The boyfriend tried the *hey, no hard feelings, man* thing a couple of times; Austin didn't even look at him. It was his own fault, anyway. His own fault. He was a fuck-up to the end. A fuck-up through-and-through. If he had just thought for a second, used his brain for a second, he would have understood, he would have realized, that all had not been lost, that even with his hands disabled he still could have gathered the tokens, he could have learned to use his feet, his toes, like the guy in that movie who painted pictures that way, he could have bent down and picked up the band-aids with his fucking teeth. If only. But he had panicked. He had spoken. He had destroyed the three trapped women's chance of redemption his own damn, stupid self.

Their voices, gentle and melancholy and musical, did not sing in his head any more. Now nothing existed inside his skull but silence.

❦

Austin's hands healed slowly. April passed, and May. The year passed, and the day. Yolanda worked Saturdays as well as weekdays at the dry cleaner's; for most of the time Austin was alone in the apartment. The boyfriend was not a live-in boyfriend, or not yet. Maybe not ever. Thad, his name turned out to be. He came over most nights, after Yolanda got off work. Sometimes they went out together. Thad and Yolanda. Not Austin. Austin sat on the couch where he also slept, when he could sleep, and sipped from the thermoses Yolanda set up for him. Soup. Juice. Tea. Through a straw, as he couldn't hold anything in either hand. Couldn't chew too well, either. Those whacks to the face hadn't done his teeth much good. Or his jaw. He wondered, sometimes, what the boyfriend thought about him living here, but if Thad had any objections, he kept them to himself.

Yolanda told Austin that he was getting better every day. She had zeal in her eyes, a missionary triumph. She'd rescued him, and she was mightily proud of herself.

"When the casts come off, I'm going to talk to Mr. Zachziewsky again about the presser job," she said. "We need another presser." He could feel her looking at him, assessingly, proprietarily, though he kept his gaze on the game show dinging and jingling on the TV in the corner. "It's not hard," she added. Austin thought that was meant to reassure him. He didn't answer her. Most of the time when Yolanda talked to him, he didn't answer. She had gotten him new clothes, she'd taken him to a barbershop for a haircut and a shave, and he'd thanked her. He thanked her when she gave him food, and he thanked her for letting him sleep on her couch, but beyond that, Austin found very little he could say to her, because he did not want to scream, and he did not want to cry. He'd cried enough in his miserable goddamn life, and it never did any good; it didn't even make him feel better. He did not want to hit her, beat on her with his casts until he broke all the little bones in both his hands all over again, and smashed her skull in. He kept quiet, most of the time, and watched TV. It wasn't hard.

One day, when Yolanda was at work, Austin stood up from the couch and went outside. He went for a walk. It was June, and it was already hot. He sweated. His hands itched inside their battered, dirty casts. He did not look down. He looked at people's faces, he looked into store windows, he paid attention to traffic lights. When he bumped into someone, he said, "Excuse me." It was a short walk. It did not make him feel better. But it wasn't hard.

A few days later, Austin took another walk. Might as well. What else did he have to do? Nothing.

There was a guy begging for change on Denby Street, a scrawny guy with long hair tied back in a ratty ponytail, filthy jeans and a leaky down vest open over layers of t-shirts. "Spare a quarter, spare a quarter," he chanted in a soft monotone. Not a good beggar, not like some other guys Austin had seen, who made eye contact and smiled and called people Sir and Ma'am and had a couple of stories to spin to catch folks' interest, to entertain them. This guy looked like he'd been on the street a while, probably a long while, but he'd never really caught on to the tricks of the trade. His face was sunken in—no back teeth, Austin thought—and his eyes were empty. His voice was low, dispirited. "Spare a quarter, spare a quarter." Passersby ignored him.

After a moment, Austin lost interest in the beggar, and began to walk on past him. Maybe he'd trudge on to Lake Street before turning back and heading home. He swung his arms a little. He had an appointment to get the casts off in a couple of weeks. Last night, Yolanda had brought up the presser job again, said the boss, Zach whatever his name was, had almost agreed to let Austin come in for an interview.

"Spare a—" the beggar's dead eyes flashed. He looked at Austin's casts, looked away, and laughed a mean, knowing laugh.

Austin stopped. Irked. Pissed, really. "What?" he snapped.

The beggar glanced back at him. A smirk slowly twisted up one side of his mouth. Suddenly he looked like a kid, the class bully dangling a wriggling worm above a girl's face. "I know you."

"You don't," Austin said, automatically.

"Yeah." He jerked his head at Austin's hands, at the casts. "You failed."

Austin jumped like he'd been poked with a cattle prod. Electricity shot through him, searing every nerve ending. Electric shame. Electric horror at being exposed. Electric terror. Almost, he turned and fled.

Almost. Austin stood his ground, though he was trembling so hard he could barely stand. He gulped. "You—"

"I watched you," the beggar said, softly. "Did you think you were the only one?" After a moment, he added, "I failed, too."

Austin looked at the quarters in the scrawny man's hand. Despite his poor technique, a few people had made donations. He thought about quarters. Less bulky than other change, easier to carry around, easier to spend in a diner or convenience store. Lots of street people asked for quarters, instead of simply change. But in addition, quarters were good for pay phones. Especially nowadays, when even a local call would set you back a dollar.

"How many?" Austin asked. "How many tried?"

The beggar shrugged, began to turn away.

"Did you call?" Austin whispered. "Three pies, plain."

The guy didn't answer, just finished turning away. He bounced the coins in the palm of his hand. "Spare a quarter, spare a quarter." His eyes were dead again, the monotone back.

Austin walked back to Yolanda's apartment. He sat on the couch.

He waited for the casts to come off his hands.

⌖

437 Carlton Street.

It was not an address he could ever forget.

It was the end of June, and the casts were off at last, but his hands were still weak and clumsy, his grip feeble, fine motor control poor. When Austin's hands had come out of their confinement, he'd thought they looked like spiders, white and thin and blind. The woman with the whirring saw told him to squeeze a rubber ball, to practice picking up pennies and toothpicks. Sure, Austin said, he'd do that.

Because his hands were still weak, he hadn't been given the presser job after all; Yolanda's boss hired his nephew who was on summer break from school. No job, no money. So one night when Yolanda and the boyfriend were out, Austin stole a couple of twenties from the slim stash she kept under the tampons in her underwear drawer before he slipped out of the apartment.

He bought three buckets of chicken from El Pollo Loco, which left him change, so he got three sodas, too.

It hurt, carrying the chicken and the drinks. His hands were always going to hurt, some days more than others, the woman with the plaster saw had said. She advised ibuprofen. Austin had thanked her.

It was a long way to Carlton Street. By the time he got there, his hands were on fire.

437.

The doors were still open, the foyer door, the inner door. Austin didn't bother ringing the bell. He turned the knob of the inner door with his wrists. The corridor was still brown, with one dim light bulb whose illumination did not reach to the end of the hall. The corridor still looked like a tunnel.

Austin walked down the tunnel. He set down the plastic bags of take-out, sucked his teeth at the pain that flared up his arms when he relaxed his hands. He stood still for a moment, just breathing, before he opened the door of apartment 1D. The apartment was dark. It smelled like an old attic. Nothing had changed.

Austin stood on the threshold and said, "Hello. I've brought you some food."

And if they did not answer him, he had already decided, he would enter anyway, grope his way in the dark, and set the food and the drink before each of the trapped women. And if they had gone, if they had been redeemed, he had already decided, he would be happy.

"Come in," someone whispered. Very softly. A thread of a voice. Then two echoes followed, *come in, come in*. Austin could not tell the voices apart. They all sounded spiritless, broken, barely alive.

"Can I have some light?"

He waited, and in time the light came, the same lamp, the same rosy glow.

Austin stepped inside. And now his heart clenched hard, and he almost cried out, because one thing was not the same. The three women had fallen further down, had sunk into the floor up to their breasts. Their arms were still free. Their heads hung limply on their necks; they did not raise their eyes to him. The big-breasted one had grown thin. The skinny one had become skeletal. The old one looked near death.

Austin set the food in front of them, opened the buckets, gave them napkins, distributed the sodas, shared out the biscuits and the potato salad that had come free with his order. The women ate slowly, listlessly, their heads hanging down, their eyes nearly shut. They did not speak.

Austin sat down on the dusty floor. He folded his hands in his lap, and waited for the women to finish their meals.

"Do you remember me?" he asked, when they were done.

"Yes," they said, though still they did not raise their eyes.

"I failed," he said, and his voice broke.

The women sighed, their breaths barely stirring the dust.

"But I want to try again," Austin said. "If you'll let me."

He waited again. He'd gotten good at waiting, lately. Austin was glad about that, glad he had something he was good at. Slowly the three women raised their heads, and he saw that their eyes were dry, and cool, and measuring.

"Let me try again," he said. "I'll do it this time. I swear."

"You swear?" the old one replied, scarcely moving her lips. Though she was almost inaudible, Austin could hear her tone of mockery. It hurt him, but then he thought: she's right. I can't swear to succeed. I can only promise to try. So he told them that.

"I promise to try."

The three women looked at each other. They looked at each other for a long time. That was okay. Austin was good at waiting, now. Then, one at a time, the three women nodded, first the skeletal one, then the one who used to have big breasts, then the oldest one. Only then did they turn their heads and look at him again.

"I will help you," Austin said, to each of them, one at a time. "I will help you. I will help you."

And the women said:

Thank you.

> *Thank you.*

> > *Thank you.*

Austin bowed his head, and his heart filled up with light, for as soon as they spoke the music returned and the inside of his skull was no longer empty. He sat still a moment, because he did not want to cry in front of them, then rose, a little stiffly, and brushed off the seat of his jeans. His hands hurt, but that was okay. He'd just bound himself to suffer again all he had suffered once already, more, probably, and in the days to come there would be times when he would despair and when he would curse himself and them and the whole fucking world, but that was okay, too.

In silence, for as soon as they had thanked him the year and the day had begun, Austin stepped forward. He went to each of the women, and one at a time, he bent low and kissed them on the cheek, the old one, the one who had once had amazing breasts, the skeletal one with the feathery hair. Then, their soft, sad, musical voices filling his head, he left apartment 1D, to embark upon his quest once more.

SHINY THING

THE NEXT TIME IT LOOKED LIKE SHE AND FRANKLIN WERE going to have a fight, Lelia hoped to hell she'd remember to check the weather forecast first. The rain had started just after breakfast. She'd heard the first drops spatter hard against the windowpanes while she was still holding on very hard to her cup of cold, untasted coffee, willing herself not to fling its contents into Franklin's face. Within a minute, the plat-plat-platting drops had turned into a torrential downpour, almost tropical in its intensity. Water cascaded down the panes in solid sheets; with all the sewer grates plugged up by that autumn's crop of fallen leaves, the street flooded quickly. And the rain went on, and went on, hour after hour, unflagging, undiminishing. Franklin, silent, avoided her, going into the bedroom to pretend to work on his dissertation when she entered the living room, rising from the computer and vanishing into the bathroom when she came into the bedroom. Lelia would have left the apartment, would have headed out into the drenching rain anyway, despite having lost her umbrella at the library, she thought, last week; she even started to get dressed, hunting for the one pair of boots she was pretty sure didn't leak too much, but it was November and it was cold, damn it. Not cold enough for snow, but cold enough that when she touched her palm to the windowpane the chill shot up to her elbow. Fuck it, she thought, this is my place just as much as it is his.

Their wedding was sixty-seven days away. When they'd finally decided on the date, Leila had set up a countdown calendar on her own computer. She'd giggled a little ruefully when she'd done it—so childish, so kid-crossing-off-the-days-until-Christmas-ish. She hadn't giggled much at the damn calendar, lately.

Lelia made more coffee, sat down at the counter in the kitchenette that was basically just one side of the living room, and rubbed the finger her engagement ring was not on. Maybe Franklin had noticed she hadn't put it back on after cleaning the bathroom last week. Maybe he'd felt hurt, and wanted to hurt her back. Unlikely, Leila thought. He hadn't even noticed she'd cleaned the bathroom.

Omar meowed.

Lelia burst into tears.

Son of a bitch, she thought, son of a bitch! She slammed the side of her fist down on the counter, making coffee slop out of her mug. Bastard, motherfucker, son of a bitch!

Omar meowed again. His ratty tail swished impatiently, and he gave Lelia his patented you-know-what-I-want-so-hop-to-it glower. "Wait," she said, but Omar had already lost patience and, muscles bunching, dropped down into a deep, preparatory crouch. "Wait!" Lelia cried, leaping off her stool to scoop the old cat up before he jumped. Omar wanted to be on the counter, his favorite spot in the apartment ever since she and he had moved in two years ago, but the four-foot leap was too much for him now. He knew it, too, and relaxed as soon as she touched him, allowing her to lift him gently and set him down, just as gently, on the countertop. Not that he was grateful; he stepped into the puddle of spilled coffee and flicked his paw angrily, and hissed when she reached for him again, hissed low in his throat with his eyes half-lidded, as if the indignity were all her fault. Omar was almost sixteen years old, and over breakfast this morning Franklin had said, casually, in the *oh, and of course* tone normal people used to bring up a topic they were certain there could be no disagreement about, that they should make the appointment with the vet at least a couple of weeks before the wedding, have it all taken care of before they got busy packing for the honeymoon. Which was supposed to be in Aruba. Which they still hadn't actually booked yet.

Lelia had sat stunned for a moment, then snapped at Franklin: *That's not fucking funny.* He'd glanced up from the journal he was reading, surprised. Puzzled. The moment Lelia realized that Franklin wasn't joking, that he thought killing her cat was not only the logical, but the inarguably correct thing to do, she'd lost her composure completely. Dizzy with disbelief, outwardly frozen and inwardly flailing at the air as she plummeted down this evil rabbit hole, Lelia tore into him. Franklin, roused, fought back, matching her viciousness for viciousness. After the first few minutes, they weren't even fighting about Omar any more, but about everything. His family, her family, his friends, her smoking, though she'd quit three months ago, his eating, which he yelled was a fucking low blow when he was working on his fucking dissertation for fuck's sake, how she didn't appreciate the pressure he was under, how she was a dilettante who could never settle on anything, how he was a pompous arrogant bastard, how the universe did so *not* revolve around his big fat hairy ass...

Eventually they'd both more or less simultaneously run out of adrenaline and invective, and an icy silence descended.

Lelia ran her hand over Omar, one long, slow stroke, then another. He arched his back and leaned into her touch, but did not purr. A sweet cat, Omar wasn't, hadn't been even in his younger days. But he was Omar, through and through. One hundred per cent Omar, even now, with his fur thinning and his knobby spine nearly poking through his skin. Lelia began to cry again, silently, a strange sort of weeping in which the tears flowed so quickly that a flurry of drops struck the countertop before she could raise her hand to her face, but in which her heart did not race, her breath did not catch in her throat. *I am perfectly calm,* she thought, *I'll stop crying in a minute.* Omar sniffed at one of the teardrops on the countertop, then licked it. Lelia looked up and saw Franklin standing a couple of feet behind her, his eyes troubled, his mouth grim.

Lelia wiped her face.

Franklin took a breath, shut his eyes, opened them again, and seemed altogether very much like a man about to say something. And now Lelia's breath caught. She blinked, flicking the last tears away, and waited, her eyes dry, a hard ache behind her breastbone.

Franklin took another breath, grimaced, and began to turn away.

The doorbell rang.

Lelia and Franklin both swung around, her toward him, him toward her, each one's glance immediately for the other in the face of this strangeness. They were not expecting anyone; they hadn't ordered delivery; outside the rain continued to pound down. Surprise and puzzlement in Franklin's gaze, and in her own as well, Lelia knew. Perhaps a touch of relief, peeking out behind Franklin's quizzically raised eyebrows, hidden behind her own quirked lip. An interruption. Something to shatter the chill silence in the apartment, or at least thaw it a little.

The doorbell rang again.

"I don't believe this," Franklin said, and Lelia rolled her eyes in agreement and actually smiled.

The apartment was on the third floor, and the living room windows faced the street. Lelia moved past Franklin, brushing by, not touching him but not avoiding him, to pull back the curtains to get a glimpse, through the driving rain, of this unexpected visitor.

The rain was still lashing down. The pane was still freezing cold; Lelia flinched as she touched her forehead to the glass. She peered out at the street. Yes, there was certainly someone standing on the stoop, and that someone was wearing an enormous, truly enormous, yellow rain slicker. No hood, no hat. The person's sparse hair was plastered to his round skull. It was the hair that made her realize it was a man. A short man, very fat, who was holding an entirely soaked-through paper grocery bag in one hand, and reaching out to press the buzzer again with the other.

"Who is it?" Franklin asked. He'd followed her to the window.

Lelia began to say she didn't know, but checked herself. She had seen him before, hadn't she? Not wearing a giant yellow rain slicker, no. In a gray suit, of unfortunate shininess, that had stretched with alarming snugness over his girth. She remembered thinking he'd looked a lot like a grounded party balloon, with his stubby arms and legs and small round head mere decorative appendages. She'd been ashamed of the cruelty of that thought. Of course she'd never say such a thing to the man's face, but still, now, she winced.

"I think you know him," she said, and moved aside as Franklin stepped forward.

He peered down, then burst out laughing. "You're kidding."

"So who is it?"

"Never saw him before in my life." Still laughing, Franklin stood on tiptoe to get a better look. "Man—guy must be nuts. Fucking hurricane out there or something, what's he thinking? He—he—" Laughter overcame language. Franklin let the curtain drop. "He looks like a beach ball."

"I saw you talking to him," Lelia said. "On the street, in front of that organic café. Havuç. Right." The short fat man had been doing the talking, actually, or so it had seemed from the end of the block. Franklin had been standing, listening, his arms crossed. She'd been late to a workshop, some Grad Center networking crap she'd attended with no real hope, only a sense of grim duty—try *everything*—so she hadn't stopped, simply glanced and hurried on.

"Never," Franklin said.

"It was last week."

Franklin shook his head, still laughing.

Lelia walked to the buzzer set high in wall, above the thermostat. She had to stretch. The people who'd lived here before must've been basketball players, she thought.

Franklin's ha-ha's cut off abruptly. "What are you doing? It's some nutcase, Lelia. No way you're letting him in."

The doorbell rang again, for the fifth or sixth time.

"He'll go away in a minute."

"What's wrong with you?" she said. "It's raining rivers, and he's soaked through. Even if he's made a mistake, wrong address, you know, he can come up here and call a cab or something."

"Don't be stupid."

Lelia mashed her finger down on the entry button, and held it there for long, long, long seconds.

"Fuck," Franklin said, with disgust. He flung himself away from the window, strode for the bedroom. As Lelia went to the apartment door and opened it, she noticed that Franklin stopped at the bedroom door. Back toward her, shoulders jigging in barely suppressed fury, still he had not vanished to his computer, not slammed a new silence between them. Her spirits lifted a bit, counteracting the anxiety in the hollow of her stomach as she listened to the short, fat man climb the stairs. His tread was slow and very heavy; she could hear his labored breathing even two flights below.

"Hello," she called. "Are you okay?"

There was no reply, except for the ponderous footfalls on the worn, lino-covered steps, and the raspy inhalations and explosive exhalations that accompanied them. Something tickled her nose; she sniffed, then let out a sharp cough. A smell was rising along with their visitor. Two smells. No, three. Wetness, naturally, wet hair and wet cloth, wet plastic and wet paper, but along with that another, greener scent, herbal, aromatic, the scent of fresh leaves, of sap, of spring; but underneath that, nearly obscured, something sickly and rotten, an aired-out sickroom smell, the odor of a washed corpse. "Franklin," she said softly, but though he had turned to face the apartment door, he stood with his arms folded and his head down, mulish and silent.

When finally the short, fat man appeared on the landing, Lelia almost cried out. He looked ill, feverish, the wetness slicking his face more sweat than rain. He was older than she had thought, long past middle-age, and the flesh of his round face had sagged off the bone to become loose, bulldog jowls. He trembled as he rested against the banister at the top of the landing, rain drops shuddering from his bright coat, a wet trail like that of a massive snail streaking the steps behind him. He still clutched the sopping grocery bag, fat fingers white on the rolled-up top; that the paper hadn't disintegrated amazed her. He's going to have a heart attack, right here on the top of the steps, Lelia thought, but the short, fat man straightened himself, met her eyes, and bobbed his head politely. "Thank you so much," he said. The scent of impossibly fresh greenery enveloped her; beneath it, the odor of illness lurked.

The wet bag was filled to bursting with something. Bursting? Burst. "Oh," the short, fat man cried, as the sides of the paper sack began, slowly but inexorably, to tear, split, and gape, "oh, oh, oh," and he swept the bag up to his chest, cradling it with a desperate tenderness, and barreled down the corridor toward her, as thunderous and unstoppable as a startled elephant. Lelia barely got out of the way. If she hadn't jumped aside, the man would have knocked her over in his rush.

"Hey," Franklin said. "What the *fuck*?"

Lelia had not gotten completely out of the short, fat man's way. The back of one of his wet hands had grazed her shoulder as he plunged into the apartment. Now something clung to her sweater, a ragged scrap of she didn't know what, limp, translucent, membranous. It had no odor. She couldn't bring herself to touch it.

Lelia shut the door.

The short, fat man had stopped in front of Franklin. Rainwater still streamed from his slicker, marking his trail, puddling around his feet. Despite the mad dash down the corridor, the man seemed to have caught his breath. "Excuse me," he said, cordially, if a bit shakily, "but I need to ask a favor."

Franklin goggled at him.

Lelia would not look at whatever it was that was stuck to her sweater. Like talking to someone with baby vomit on her shoulder, she figured. You had to pretend it wasn't there. Little harder when it was your shoulder, but still doable. Her stomach fluttered. Dammit, she could do this. She'd had lots of practice at ignoring things. "Can we help you?" she asked.

The man turned slightly, bobbed his head, then looked back at Franklin. The paper grocery sack in his arms, Lelia now saw, was stuffed full of leaves, dark green and glossy, each about as large as her hand. As soon as she'd shut the door, the smell of them had begun to fill the apartment.

On the kitchenette counter, Omar lashed his tail furiously.

"A cab," muttered Franklin. "A cab, right? Yeah. The phone's over there."

"Young man," the short, fat man, who was sweating quite profusely, said, "I am very sorry to impose on you. But could you please take this," he ducked his chin at the bundle of leaves, "to its destination? I am afraid that... that I may not be able to complete the journey myself."

"What the—" Franklin caught himself. "What are you talking about? Who are you? I don't even know you."

"You were talking to him in front of that café," Lelia said, and again the short, fat man bobbed his head at her.

"No, I was not," Franklin snapped.

"Please, won't you sit down?" Lelia said, because the man was looking not at all well. He'd turned away from her again, but in the brief glimpse she'd gotten of his full face, it appeared as if his cheeks were melting. He'd also begun to tremble again.

"Please," he said. "There isn't much time. It must be now. There is a little alley, very narrow, and only one street long, on Allern Avenue, between the hardware store— regretfully, that establishment's name has slipped my memory—and Natella's Vintage Boutique." A leaf escaped from the widening rift in the bottom of the paper sack and glided to the floor. Then another. The short, fat man looked down in consternation. "Please. Do you understand the destination? Allern Avenue—"

"You're fucking crazy," Franklin said.

Let me get you a glass of water, Lelia was about to say, but then it struck her as painfully ridiculous to offer water to a man so sopping wet. Tea, she would offer him tea, then, but before she could, the final fibers of the bag gave way, and the whole load of leaves tumbled out, cascading down his legs and over his feet, spilling across the floor. A few fluttered down on top of Franklin's sweat-sock covered toes. He yelled, "Shit!" and jumped back as if from an electric shock.

From behind Lelia there came a loud thud. *Oh no*, she thought, her heart in her mouth; for months now this had been her nightmare, getting distracted and letting Omar hurt himself, or being gone from the apartment when the dumb cat forgot he was old and launched himself off the counter the way he used to. Returning to find him with legs snapped, hips dislocated, skull cracked.

But not this time, not yet. Omar stalked into the living room, fur bristling and eyes alert and wild. He stared at the short, fat man, who wiped his face with a shaky hand and then bobbed his head at Omar. Omar sniffed at one of the fallen leaves, then went into that stoned-looking thing cats did when they wanted to get a good whiff of something, that open-mouthed, slit-eyed huffing that drew scent into the deepest recesses of the feline olfactory system. Omar sneezed. Then he blinked and padded off to the bedroom, tail erect. Franklin swore under his breath.

"I'll get another bag," Lelia said. "We'll pick everything up."

"Thank you so much," the man whispered.

Lelia opened the cupboard under the sink; squatting, she sorted through their hefty collection of bags. A big one, with handles, would be good. Plastic, or plasticized, to keep out the rain, which was still bucketing down. The wind had picked up, too; she could hear it howling outside, whipping the telephone wires, lashing the already bare trees. It would be next to impossible to get a cab to come out in this weather.

When she straightened up, big university bookstore bag in hand, she saw that the man had sat down on the floor. "Are you all right?" she asked again, but the drips inching down his cheeks and his hands were no longer water, if they ever had been only water. "What's in the alley?" she asked. "A friend," he said. "A friend in need." He winced at the sight of the plastic bag, but nodded, and together he and Lelia began to gather up the fallen leaves. They were soft, like old paper, and so green and new she feared they'd stain her fingers. The short, fat man handled the leaves very carefully, but with swiftness; Lelia, enveloped in the scent of an impossible forest, moved more slowly.

"Where do they come from?" she asked. "What are they for?" but the man, breathing hard, shook his head slightly and did not answer.

"Put your shoes on," she said to Franklin, who let out an incredulous laugh. She could have slapped him; would have, if she had thought it would have done any good.

"I know where Allern Avenue is," she said. The man did not glance at her, but gazed steadily at Franklin. "Does it have to be him?" Lelia asked. "Why?"

"Okay," Franklin said, with an air of decisiveness. "I'm calling a cab. Sorry for your troubles, man, you know, and sorry it's raining like a bitch, but you're out of here."

"Have to," the man murmured. "No, it doesn't have to be. Really, there is no have to."

"How do you know him?"

"I don't. I spoke to him just the once. I believed... but perhaps I was wrong."

At the phone, Franklin cursed, then began to punch out another number.

"What's going to happen to you?" Lelia asked, for the skin had quite completely sloughed off the man's face, and the flesh of his hands was dissolving; she could see the glint of bone.

He smiled at her weakly.

Lelia got another bag from under the sink and stuck in inside the bookstore bag, tucking it over the leaves. Not waterproof, not even close, but then the paper sack the man had been carrying certainly hadn't been waterproof, and when she had picked up the soft, floppy leaves from the floor, they had been as dry as the insides of ancient library books. Lelia wondered what would happen if she tore off a small, a tiny, fragment of one leaf and ate it.

"Allern Avenue," the short, fat man whispered.

"I know," Lelia said. "I understand." She went into the bedroom to get changed. Omar, from atop the pillows, watched her benignly. After she'd laced up her boots, Lelia stroked him. This time, he began to purr. "Bastard," she whispered. "Don't die, okay? Just don't die." Omar's tail twitched; eyes shut, he continued to purr, even after she'd straightened up, hastily blown her nose, and left the bedroom.

Franklin watched with disbelief as she put on her coat and found a serviceable hat. "There's no cabs," he said. "Nobody's coming out."

"I figured that."

The short, fat man looked very weary. Beneath him, on the floor, spreading out from under the flaps of his bright yellow slicker, a wide wetness grew. Franklin hadn't noticed yet.

"You're going to get soaked," he said. "You'll get sick."

Soaked, certainly. The hard nugget of anger behind her breastbone, the diamond of fury that had ached there since breakfast, burned hot. "Take care of him while I'm gone," she said. "You can do that at least, can't you?"

"What?" Franklin said, and again she could have hit him.

"I'm not in need of anything," the short, fat man murmured. "But please, hurry. It must be now."

Lelia picked up the bulging bookstore bag with its dumb convenience store plastic bag shielding its contents. Light, of course. It held only leaves. She'd have to hold on to it hard, outside, fight the wind for it, as she made her way to Allern Avenue. "I'm going. Do I need to do anything else? Just bring this there? Do I have to put it anywhere special?"

"Just bring it. That is enough."

"Okay. I'll be back as soon as I can."

The man nodded.

"You're leaving him here?" Franklin yelped. "Fucking shit, Lee, no way! I want his crazy ass out of here!"

"Does he look like he can walk, Franklin?" she said quietly. The diamond of anger flared hotter. "Does he look like he can even stand the fuck up?" She stared at Franklin until he flicked his gaze away. "Make him some tea. Make him some damn soup. Give him a blanket. *Do* something."

Lelia went to the door. Behind her, the man murmured, "I thank you very kindly." She didn't bother with an umbrella. With the wind, it would be useless, and with the wind, she'd need both hands to hold on to the bag. Now, as she was about to leave, Lelia felt a sudden, icy fear, but she closed the apartment door firmly, and headed down the stairs without looking back.

Later, she would think about that journey in the rain at the oddest times. Not during a thunderstorm or summer downpour. The trip did not leave her with a fear of rain, or even any special alertness to it. Instead, memories of the drenching trek, the instant sopping of her clothes, the battle with the wind, would come to her in calm, warm moments, on the beach, in the sunshine, on a quiet bus, in a deserted museum, or alone in her bed.

It was dark outside, dark because of the storm and because it was now late afternoon. The city was empty, everyone indoors, no cars, no pedestrians; stores were shuttered, kiosks locked up. Water ruled; Lelia had to wade across flooded intersections, dodge backed-up, gushing sewers. Water streamed from above; her hat did not shield her, her coat did not protect her. She trudged, she waded, she splashed, head down, arms around the bag. She knew where Allern Avenue was. She knew the hardware store, and she knew the vintage clothes boutique. She'd never noticed the alley the short, fat man had claimed was located between them, but she had no doubt it was there. Or, at least, was there today, would be there when she reached it.

It was.

Narrow, as he had said, so narrow her shoulders scraped the walls on either side. Franklin would have had to go in edgewise, if he had come. Dark, too; Lelia inched into the darkness, cautious toes advancing, encountering no obstacle. No garbage in the alley. That might have been the weirdest thing yet. She wondered if she should call out, announce herself. *I'm here, I've brought...* Her exploring foot met a barrier. Slowly, Lelia leaned her head forward until her brow met stone. A wall, running with water, but not as cold as her windowpane had been. She shuffled backwards one pace, bent, and set down the bag. Was this right? Was this what she was supposed to do? She didn't know, but could think of nothing else. To bring it and to leave it, that was all she had been charged with, right? Rain beat down on her back, sharply focused by the narrow walls. Backwards still, with slow, nervous steps, Lelia withdrew from the alley.

Out again, free, standing in the full force of the wind and the downpour, Lelia took a shaky breath. She didn't know whether to laugh or cry. Then something came rolling out of the alley, something swift and bright and flashing, and she almost screamed.

The flashing thing came to a halt, and its brightness settled down into a glow, and then a simple shininess. It would fit into her palm easily, and it looked smooth and... warm. For me? Lelia thought, with wonderment. Could this shiny thing possibly be for me?

She held her breath, and picked it up. It did indeed fit neatly into the palm of her hand. It was hard, and smooth, and warm, and it continued to shine with a quiet, confident radiance.

What on earth it was, what on earth it was for, Lelia had no idea.

When she got home, she was not surprised to find that the man was gone. The floor in the living room was wet, but not from him; Franklin had mopped it. The odor of pine cleaner, acrid and artificial, had chased the scent of the leaves out of the apartment.

Franklin was watching TV.

Omar came padding out of the bedroom, giving Lelia his *I'm starving* glare. Lelia opened up a can for him, even before stripping off her sopping clothes. Not that Omar appreciated it. A sweet cat he wasn't. Never had been.

Lelia waited until Franklin finally switched off the television before showing him the shiny thing.

He didn't ask her what it was. He didn't wonder where it came from. He knew. He put one hand to his chest. The blood drained from his face. Lelia had never before seen a person look so bereft.

They gazed at each other in silence, she in rightful possession of a treasure she had no clue what to do with, he in shock at his loss. She could see the emptiness opening up inside him, the hollow space that would never be filled, and though she had her own worries, for no treasure ever came without pain, Lelia knew for certain that even in her uncertainty, she was much better off than Franklin would ever be.

Frank, and Stephanie, and Jimmy Popcorn

All right, settle down.

Now, you all know that in the long ago, before the sun was yellow and the rain became sweet, things were different. People had names like Stephanie and Frank and Jimmy Popcorn, and plastic was nearly as valuable as water. Sometimes it's hard to tell a made-up tale from a true story of the long ago, but the true stories are history. They tell us how things used to be.

You've all heard of the Endless Land. That was a real place. Still is, though it has a different name now. You know The City of New Unity City? Right, tiny little place. But it was built square in the middle of where the Endless Land used to be. What happened to the rest of the Endless Land? Office parks, mostly. They have a museum there, though, full of stuff from the long ago. You should visit it sometime. Very educational.

Stephanie and Frank and Jimmy Popcorn are not in the museum, but then lots of people who really lived never make it into museums. Do you think any of you are going to be in a museum one day? I wouldn't bet on it.

All right. In the long ago, when people had names like Stephanie and Frank and Jimmy Popcorn, three people named Stephanie and Frank and Jimmy Popcorn made a trip to the Endless Land. Back then, you couldn't just push your thumb against a strip at the depot and have a ticket pop out of the machine. A trip was something special. You had to plan it. Pack for it. Exercise until your body was strong enough to endure the stress of travel. Take medicine so you wouldn't get sick. Make a will so if you died on the road, people back home would know what to do with your stuff.

Many people traveled to the Endless Land, because they were following stories. All the stories we have now about that place? There were even more back then. A lot were made-up stories. In the Endless Land, everybody was beautiful. Now, you know that one wasn't true. There are beautiful people and ugly people and people in-between, and there always were and always will be. In the Endless Land, everybody was happy. Come on, how many of you think that was a true telling? Just imagine that, a place where everyone is happy all the time. Pretty scary, yah? Gotta be thinking psychoactives in the water, or some powerful delusion spell. No, I didn't mean illusion. We're going to have to work on vocabulary, you guys. In the Endless Land, birds talked and fish sang, and the grass seeds jumped onto your skin and burrowed down to sprout from spaces between your bones. I'm not going to say a word about birds or fish, but most people who did a little studying before they set off on their trip knew they should pay attention to the grass.

The grass told you where to dig.

In some of the stories, it says that people who came back—or didn't come back, just sent a postcard or email or something—said or wrote something like this: *The grass made us dig.* I'll tell you right now and flat out that wasn't so. The grass only waved its little blades and pointed, like. Or turned colors, sometimes, for people who could perceive the significance of shades. Rustled, too, I suppose. It's not hard to believe rustling. But grass never grew in people's bones, and it never made a single solitary human being do anything. Gave hints, that's all.

All that grass is gone, now. Office parks, like I said. There's no grass in office parks. Sometimes there are trees, but that's not the same thing. Besides, the trees in office parks are kept in cages. Safer that way. Trees hold grudges.

Nice to look at, I guess, but I for one wouldn't want to sit on a bench underneath one of them, cage or no cage.

Stephanie and Frank and Jimmy Popcorn met on the road. They all came from different townlands, and had all started out from different directions. They met up at a motel just inches from where the Endless Land began. A lot of people stopped there, to rest and build up their strength and courage for the last stage of the trip. It was autumn, height of the travel season, and the motel was swollen with guests. There was only one room left. Stephanie and Frank and Jimmy Popcorn glared at each other across their luggage. Now, the story goes that Stephanie was the biggest, with muscles like those of a person who stacked crates for a living, and she folded her arms and stared at the other two with an expression that said, Yours wouldn't be the first throats I've cut. Frank was the oldest, with a big bald spot on the back of his head, and the least amount of luggage. He used to work as a waiter in a small lunch-stop café, and he'd decided on the voyage to the Endless Land after he lost his job and his husband had run off with a younger man. Jimmy Popcorn was just barely grown, with long hair he kept tied back with a bit of red string, and clothes that had been out of style for a decade or two. None of them smiled, and that made them all members of the same tribe. It took them a few moments to realize this.

Jimmy Popcorn spoke first. "I think we're all here for the same thing."

People traveled to the Endless Land for many reasons, but most of the reasons boiled down a single desire—to find a flake or drop or shard-sliver of hope. It's true that some folks came greedy, or got greedy once they'd arrived, and started digging shafts, seeking whole nuggets or chunks or even veins of the stuff, but they usually wound up caught by the digging, shoveling and drilling deeper and deeper into the land, losing all memory of why they'd stuck a spade in the dirt in the first place, so that the digging became everything. Those folks rarely made it back from the Endless Land. Their bones are still there, under the poured concrete of the office parks.

"I wish I hadn't come," Frank said. "I don't have any money left, and I don't think I have the strength to walk another step."

"When's the last time you smiled?" Jimmy Popcorn asked.

Frank shook his head. "I can't remember."

"You?"

Stephanie kept glaring. "Never."

"All right, then," said Jimmy Popcorn. And though he was the youngest of them, and wore ridiculous clothes, Frank and Stephanie waited to hear what he would say next. "Let's share the room, and set out together in the morning."

Hope grew in the Endless Land, underground. Nowadays, we have to dig it out from beneath our own skins. The hospitals are full of people whose hands weren't very steady with their knives, or who used the wrong type of knife. It has to be an ice-knife, but you all know that. In the long ago, you could dig it out from the earth, if you listened to the grass and followed its signs. In the museum in The City of New Unity City, there are a few chips and shreds of hope on display, in a locked cabinet. They don't look like much. Pale gray flecks, indigo crumbs. They don't glitter, or anything like that. They don't shine, or vibrate, or turn warm in your hand. If you don't read the card on the cabinet, you might not even realize what they are.

Stephanie said, "So we are No-smiles. So what? That doesn't make us friends."

"It makes us kin."

"Only travel-kin."

"All I suggested was sharing the room." Jimmy Popcorn had no smiles in him, but his eyes were warm.

Frank nodded. "We could get out of the cold, at least."

"Fine," Stephanie said, angrily. "But you two stay out of my way."

People got like that sometimes, when their whole lives had ticked away without ever a smile or dust-mote of hope. Still do.

They went back into the motel, and took the room. There was one bed; Jimmy Popcorn said Frank should take it, as he was the oldest, and the most exhausted. He and Stephanie lay on the floor. Apart, naturally. They talked, occasionally, as they rested, because it's hard to sleep in a strange place, with strange people, even if you're very tired. First it was about ordinary things, what townland they came from, where they'd gone to school, what food from home they missed most. Then, because they were travel-kin, and all No-smiles, they started telling their secrets. Travel-kin do that. They pretty much can't help themselves.

In any case, it passed the time. In the morning, Stephanie bought them all breakfast. The glare had gone from her, but she moved like someone underwater. Like she was thinking hard, and the thinking was taking most of her strength. Frank felt better; he had a map in his backpack, and he took it out and showed it to the others. Jimmy Popcorn washed his face with motel soap, and said, "We'll follow the map, but we must pay attention to the grass."

Stephanie's secret was that she cried every time she woke up.

Frank's secret was that it hurt him in the heart whenever he heard music.

Jimmy Popcorn's secret was that he was afraid of the sky. They had medicine for that, even in the long ago, but he'd tried it and it hadn't worked for him.

If I could smile when I wake up, Stephanie thought, I could get through my days with so much less pain.

If I could smile when I heard music, Frank thought, my heart could be at peace.

If I could smile at the sky, Jimmy Popcorn thought, I could do so much more with my life.

They set out. The people who lived in the Endless Land were used to travelers and questers; nobody looked at them twice. The Endless Land, in the long ago, stretched far and wide in all directions, so there was plenty of room to move around. Tourists didn't bump into each other much, and it was easy for the locals to ignore them.

Frank's map turned out to be of little value, which surprised no one, not even Frank. Stephanie strode ahead, like a general. Jimmy Popcorn kept his eyes down, watching the grass.

Many people traveled to the Endless Land and never found what they were looking for. It wasn't that what they were looking for didn't exist. In the long ago, the Endless Land had everything. What happened was that people got distracted, sidetracked, discouraged. They ran out of patience, or they ran out of time, or they ran out of money, and gave up. I'm not including the greedy ones here, who became trapped in the pits they dug. That was completely their own fault.

Travel-kin, if they're together long enough, and especially if they're of the same tribe, can find themselves growing toward each other, without even realizing it, becoming family-kin. Frank and Stephanie and Jimmy Popcorn trekked over the Endless Lands together for a long time. Stephanie paid for their food. Frank told jokes. Jimmy Popcorn rubbed their feet when they were too tired to take another step. Helplessly, hopelessly, the way these things happened, they glanced around one day and discovered that they all loved each other.

Jimmy Popcorn was the youngest, and the jumpiest—because of the sky, you know—and Stephanie and Frank treated him a little bit like a baby brother you need to have a lot of patience with, but when he said, "I see the grass pointing," they both stopped, and followed him, even though neither could see what Jimmy Popcorn said he saw, and when he knelt down and ran his fingers across a patch of grass that looked exactly the same as every other patch of grass, then took his spoon (for he had traveled with a spoon, and nothing more, to dig with) and began to delve, Frank and Stephanie knelt on either side of him and drew out their spades. They had known before starting out that they had to take care against becoming miners; neither of them had brought shovels or picks. That was smart, yah?

They only had to dig down a short way, only had to kneel and scrape and scoop for a few minutes, before one of them uncovered a sliver of a smile. It was slender and fragile, no thicker than a loop of thread. Very easy to overlook such a thing, in all the dirt and stones and roots and worms, you'd think. What color was it? I couldn't tell you. Probably dirt-colored, like most things in the ground.

Now, it could be that Jimmy Popcorn saw it first, and it was Stephanie's smile. It could be Stephanie turned over a little clod of earth and touched it and knew at once what she'd found, and it was Frank's smile. In any event, they'd discovered one, and there were three of them.

Stephanie picked the smile up, and laid it out across her palm. They all looked at it, then they all looked at each other. It could be that if this had happened the first day they'd started out together, they'd have squabbled or fought, hit each other with their spades and spoons, or their fists. It could be that this would have been the case if they'd found the smile the previous day, even. But this is what happened *that* day.

Stephanie stretched the thread-thin treasure over her hand. It barely reached from one side of her palm to the other. "Frank," she said, "have you got a knife?"

Frank didn't.

Jimmy Popcorn gave her his spoon. Somehow, with all the digging, his spoon had become very sharp. Unexpected things like that used to happen all the time in the Endless Land.

Stephanie cut the smile into three pieces, as equal in size as she could manage. She allowed Jimmy Popcorn first choice, and Frank the second. Then the three of them took their pieces of smile and touched them to their lips, and the little pieces grew and flowed and entered into them and rooted deep, big enough and strong enough to last for the rest of their lives.

People used to be able to do that. Did you know people used to be able to do that? It's hard for us to understand now the way the world was then. But once people could not only find hope and smiles and love buried in the earth of the Endless Land, but share one little bit among three.

All that went away when the Endless Land ended, and we have to live in the world we have now. But it's important to remember that the world wasn't always the way it is now.

What happened to Frank and Stephanie and Jimmy Popcorn? They went home, of course. And now you all get home, too. Shut the door behind you. And put your smiles on. You think the grannies made them for you to keep them in your pockets?

Ah, lovely smiles. As beautiful as sweet rain, or the warm yellow of the sun.

I hope you all remember to thank your grannies, and to honor their scars.

Travel with kindness, and keep your smiles alight. Our world is hard, but there is still beauty in it.

PATRICIA RUSSO had her first professional short story, "True Love", published in 1987 in the anthology *Women of Darkness: Original Horror and Dark Fantasy by Contemporary Women Writers*, edited by Kathryn Ptacek. Since then her work has appeared in *Lone Star Stories, Electric Velocipede, Abyss and Apex, Talebones, Tales of the Unanticipated, Not One of Us*, in the anthologies *Corpse Blossoms* and *Zencore*, and in many other fine publications. She is that rarest of authors: she has no website, no blog, nothing on the internet to indicate that she even exists — except for a trail of fiction that reveals the prolific and generous writer behind the name. *Shiny Thing* is her first short story collection.

CPSIA information can be obtained at www.ICGtesting.com
Printed in the USA
BVOW050626210911

271725BV00004B/14/P